GUARDIANS
of GA'HOOLE

The River of Wind

D0972725

ENJOY ALL OF THE BOOKS IN
THE GUARDIANS *of* GA'HOOLE SERIES!

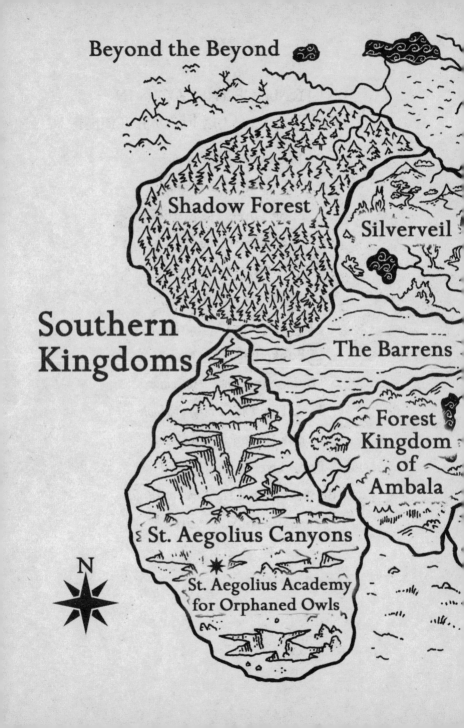

She set the glass down on the torn piece of parchment.
"Now tell me, what do you see?"

GUARDIANS
of GA'HOOLE
THE LEGENDS

BOOK THIRTEEN

The River of Wind

BY KATHRYN LASKY

SCHOLASTIC INC.

New York Toronto London Auckland Sydney
Mexico City New Delhi Hong Kong Buenos Aires

No part of this publication may be reproduced, or stored in a retrieval system, or transmitted in any form or by any means, electronic, mechanical, photocopying, recording, or otherwise, without written permission of the publisher. For information regarding permission, write to Scholastic Inc., Attention: Permissions Department, 557 Broadway, New York, NY 10012.

ISBN-13: 978-0-439-88807-3
ISBN-10: 0-439-88807-7

Text copyright © 2007 by Kathryn Lasky.

Illustrations copyright © 2007 by Scholastic Inc. All rights reserved. Published by Scholastic Inc. SCHOLASTIC and associated logos are trademarks and/or registered trademarks of Scholastic Inc.

Design by Steve Scott

12 11 10 9 8 7 6 5 4 3 2   7 8 9 10 11 12/0

Printed in the U.S.A.   40

First printing, July 2007

Northern Kingdoms

Glauxian Brothers
Retreat

Bitter
Sea

Kiel Bay

Stormfast Island

Bay of Fangs

Everwinter Sea

Ice Talons

Ice
Narrows

Dark Fowl Island

Southern
Kingdoms

Contents

Prologue

Threading through the roar of the waterfall, the scratch of a pen on parchment could be heard. Heard, that is, if there was anyone to listen except for the writer. But there wasn't. Most couldn't stand the fall's noise. Some said it made them deaf. But Bess, a Boreal Owl, was apparently immune. Her hearing was as sharp as the night she had arrived at the waterfall some years before to lay the bones of her father, Grimble, under the hood of the bell in the tower. Among Boreal Owls it was thought that if such an owl died beneath the clapper of a bell, or if its bones could be put to rest there, then its scroom would go straight to glaumora. Was it a myth? An old story half-believed, half-scoffed at? A superstition? Who was to judge? The Boreals believed it.

Bess wrote:

My Dearest Otulissa,

It has been a long time since we have communicated or you have visited me here in the Palace of Mists. I have been in a deep study of — or should I say "lost in"? — what we call "The Elsewhere." But now I am found, or rather I have found some astonishing documents pertaining to this region where the stars configure themselves into constellations we have never seen in the Five Kingdoms. As you know, until this time I had uncovered precious little documentation of The Elsewhere. Only star maps. I had always assumed that these were the creations of the Others — their astronomers and cartographers. But such is not the case. . . .

CHAPTER ONE

Astonishing – Absolutely Astonishing

Otulissa inhaled sharply, and reread the sentence. *But such is not the case. These star maps were not created by the Others, but by owls. There is in fact a sixth kingdom of owls. It is called the Middle Kingdom, and I believe it is within wingreach.* The parchment trembled as Otulissa read. She could not keep her talons still. "This is absolutely incredible," she whispered to herself. "Another kingdom of owls — but where? How?" For centuries — millennia — it was thought there were only five owl kingdoms. Six! Since when? Why had no one heard of it before now? And it was within wingreach! One could fly there!

How could that be? The Elsewhere was across the vastest of oceans. She read on: *About a year ago, I discovered a deep recess in the library here that I had not even known existed. It had been concealed purposely behind a false wall, it turned out, constructed with some sort of clay and wattle at the back of an almost empty section of the library. The wall looked more like an ill-made bird's nest, a seagull-type of construction, or perhaps even a pack rat's cache. It wasn't.*

Do you remember the slight earthquake we had many moon cycles ago? Well, apparently it loosened the wattle and stones. For it was after the quake that I discovered the recess and in it what appeared to be fragments of parchment and scraped skins — perhaps mole or even lemming, the kind of coverings that the ancient owls often used to protect writings. They were not books such as the Others had left here in this library. These were fragments of writings, badly damaged and barely decipherable, but nonetheless, I could tell immediately that they were not the writings of the Others. It was not handwriting, but bore the distinct marks of a talon, perhaps more than one talon. I cannot even begin to describe to you the tumult in my gizzard. I suspect you might be feeling something of this now as you read this letter. . . .

"To put it mildly," Otulissa muttered to herself.

I am not sure how these fragments got here. From studying the talon writing, I sense there was more than one writer, but not many. Perhaps there were traveling scholars in those days who flew here from this distant kingdom to exchange information — but with whom? I know you must wonder why I have waited so long to write you about this discovery. First, I was not exactly sure what I had discovered. I kept hoping that I might find more. I found very little.

And then, quite honestly, I was not sure what the existence of another kingdom, the sixth kingdom, would mean for our world. We have, after all, just come through a bad time — the Guardians in particular — with that dark period of the Golden Tree, the terrible arrests, and then the Battle in the Beyond with Nyra. We all hope she is gone, but do we know with any real certainty? What would she make of the news of yet another kingdom? I felt that it was best to wait. But I have waited long enough.

Otulissa shook her head violently. It seemed suddenly that her brain was too small to accommodate this bizarre idea. A sixth kingdom? But she was compelled to read on.

I feel that it is imperative that you and the Band and, yes, possibly even the Chaw of Chaws, come immediately to the Palace of Mists. I do not want to elaborate any further about what I have learned is called the Middle Kingdom. Because of the uncertainty surrounding Nyra and the condition of her troops, I feel that news of this kingdom must be kept absolutely secret. The rest must know nothing until we decide what to do. Destroy this letter immediately upon reading it.

Your dear friend, Bess

Otulissa read the letter once more, committing it to memory, and then held it over the flame of the small fire in the grate of her hollow. She watched, transfixed, as the edges of the parchment singed a tawny amber, then began to curl. There was a crackling, followed by a small burst of devouring flames. The parchment blackened and then there were only ashes. She took a small metal rod and poked at them, making sure that no legible pieces had survived. Satisfied, she went to her cupboard and poured a small drop of bingle juice into a nut cup — a rare act for Otulissa — then did a short hop to the window ledge of her hollow and peered into the day. While the rest of the tree slept peacefully, outside it was wild and blustery. It was that cusp between winter and spring that could bring any kind of weather. *But thank Glaux*, Otulissa thought as she looked out, *the Great Ga'Hoole Tree looks normal.* "Normal" meant that its branches were bare of leaves, and the vines of milkberries were white, as they should be in these, the last stages of winter, the season of the White Rain. There was the faintest glimmer of silver in the berries, indicating that spring would be coming soon.

Recently, the tree had been strangely afflicted, and although the seasons changed, the tree did not. The milkberries had remained the same bright golden hue of summer — through autumn, winter, and spring. It had not only been the tree that had been affected, but most of its inhabitants as well. The Band, with young King Coryn, had been away on a long journey. In their absence, the ember, which Coryn had retrieved, became an object of worship for many in the tree. The Guardians of Ga'Hoole had forgotten their owl ways and become quite ... quite Other-ish. It sent a tremor through Otulissa's gizzard to remember it. She herself had been imprisoned for "blaspheming the ember."

Glaux! she thought. The brainpower that had been wasted — absolutely squandered — on contriving countless silly rituals surrounding the ember. Anyone who dared to question the rituals was immediately arrested. A prison — an actual prison! — had been constructed in one of the hollows, and Bubo had been fooled into making bars for it in his forge. Was there anything more un-Ga'Hoolian than prison bars! The true bars were on the minds of the Guardians who had conceived such a thing! Those owls were gone now. Not imprisoned, but "retired" to various Glauxian retreats in the Northern Kingdoms. The tree had been restored to rights, and the ember had been sequestered away where it would never again become an object of such outrageous idolatry. Its peculiar powers, if not exactly lessened, were at least better understood: It was now realized that the ember was neither purely good nor purely evil.

Otulissa took a tiny sip from the nut cup and felt her

gizzard calm as she looked out into the sleet-slashed day. The branches tossed wildly and the entire tree gave an occasional moan. The milkberry vines tangled in the wind. *Dirty weather.* The kind that old Ezylryb liked to take the weather-interpretation chaw out in — supposedly for instructional purposes, but really just for a great ride. There were always seagulls out on this kind of a day, full of foul language and dirty jokes to match the weather. And no one had enjoyed a dirty joke more than the legendary old ryb Ezylryb.

But her mind was wandering. She had to inform the Band. *A sixth kingdom!* Astonishing — absolutely astonishing. She had better go and wake them up. But should she wake the king? No one except the Band, herself, and the late Ezylryb knew about the Palace of Mists. But Bess was now suggesting that the Chaw of Chaws — which included Martin and Ruby, who knew nothing of Bess or the Palace — should come to this secret place. The Chaw of Chaws was probably the most efficient combat unit in the history of owls. Their combination of talents, which ranged from superb flying abilities to colliering skills and deftness with battle claws, made them a formidable fighting force. But their real power did not come from any one specific weapon or skill but rather from their uncanny ability to work together.

"Chaw of Chaws," Otulissa whispered to herself. She would ask Soren who should be informed and when. Despite her resolve to stay calm, her gizzard was seized by a sudden swirling agitation at the very thought of a new kingdom — a new world!

CHAPTER TWO

Otulissa Breaks the News

From outside Soren's hollow Otulissa heard movements. *What's he doing up at this time of day?* she wondered. She knew that Soren's chicks, Bell, Bash, and Blythe — the three B's, as they had come to be called — were off with their aunt Eglantine, her friend Primrose, and their mum, Pelli, on their first training mission. A forest fire in Silverveil afforded an opportunity for teaching the colliering, search-and-rescue, and tracking chawlets, which were groups of young owls in training before it was decided to which chaw they were best suited. Pelli was now ryb of search-and-rescue and was off leading one of the chawlets. Soren must have been lonely without them, Otulissa thought, but he put up a good front.

"Soren?" Otulissa tapped lightly on the edge of the entry port and peeked in.

"Otulissa! What brings you here this time of the day? Why aren't you asleep?"

"I might ask the same of you."

"Yes, well . . . with Pelli and the young'uns gone, I rattle around in here like a loose milkberry. It's hard to sleep, you know."

"Well, I'm afraid my news will not help," Otulissa said matter-of-factly.

"Oh, Glaux, what is it now?"

"It's not bad news — no, not at all." She hesitated. "It's just . . . rather astonishing."

A perplexed light flashed deep within Soren's black eyes. "What is it?"

"It's rather unbelievable, really."

Soren had never seen Otulissa so tentative. Almost at a loss for words, although that was unimaginable. The Spotted Owl was always so talkative. "Soren, I have had word from Bess," she finally said.

"Written in the usual code?"

"Yes, of course. We always use the code." Otulissa exhaled with a great *whoosh*. "Soren, Bess thinks there is a sixth owl kingdom."

"Whhhhhhaaaat?" Soren staggered on his perch.

"She thinks there is another kingdom of owls."

"She *thinks*? Does she *know*? Where? How?"

"I think she knows," Otulissa replied.

"You *think* she *knows*? What in hagsmire does that mean?"

"Well, I know she knows. She didn't want to elaborate on it in the letter — even in code. I had to destroy it as soon as I read it. But she has evidence."

"Evidence? What kind of evidence?" Soren blinked rapidly.

"Fragments of documents, apparently. Just let me recite the letter to you."

Soren looked around nervously. "Come to the back of the hollow and keep your voice low."

Soren listened quietly and then asked her to repeat it. "Now say that part about the star maps again."

"These star maps," Otulissa reiterated, *"were not created by the Others, but by owls. There is in fact a sixth kingdom of owls. It is called the Middle Kingdom. . . . About a year ago, I discovered . . . fragments of writings, badly damaged and barely decipherable, but nonetheless, I could tell immediately that they were not the writings of the Others. It was not handwriting, but bore the distinct marks of a talon, perhaps more than one talon,"* she recited a bit more.

Soren ran a talon through his port wing feathers, a habit of his when thinking deeply. "She can really tell that there was more than one owl who wrote this stuff, eh?"

"Yes, she's very good at that sort of thing," Otulissa replied softly.

"Bess is good at a lot of things. She thinks that these

owls might have been some sort of scholars trading in information the way Trader Mags trades in goods?"

Otulissa sniffed haughtily. "Well, it's hard to use the words 'Trader Mags' and 'scholars' in the same sentence — but basically, yes."

"Curious idea, isn't it? Itinerant scholar-owls," Soren mused.

"Strictly hypothetical, of course. I mean, she couches her supposition in all sorts of very conditional language." Otulissa was back to her old academic self. Big words, convoluted, scholarly surmises, and interpretations. It was enough to drive one yoicks.

"Otulissa!" Soren said somewhat sharply. "Here's something that's not so hypothetical. Sometime in the past owls from a sixth kingdom have come here. Therefore, I would say that they were more advanced than we are. I mean, our ancestors didn't even know of its existence, much less go there. And who knows what was involved crossing a sea so vast that we have never even bothered to name it. For centuries, owls of the Five Kingdoms have called it the Unnamed Sea."

Otulissa blinked. There was no owl like Soren for cutting so directly to the chase, she thought.

"Well, we need to tell the Band and Coryn," Soren said, his black eyes sparkling now.

"But does Coryn know about Bess and the Palace of Mists?"

"Well..." Soren began somewhat sheepishly. "You know when we went on that trip before all that ember-worship nonsense? We were hollowed up with bad weather in Silverveil. You know how you can get stuck there. We began telling stories."

"Yes, I remember. A male-bonding thing no doubt," Otulissa huffed.

Soren suddenly swelled up. "Male bonding, my talon! How can you say that! Gylfie was there." He stomped on his perch. "Anyway, that's when we told Coryn about Bess and the palace. He was fascinated."

"Who wouldn't be?" Otulissa said in a somewhat more conciliatory tone. "All right, it makes sense that he should go. If there is a sixth kingdom ... well, it's logical that our own king should know about it."

"Yes." Soren nodded firmly and blinked. "I think I should gather the rest of the Chaw of Chaws and take them to Coryn's hollow at once." He hopped off his perch and lighted down on the rim and looked out. "It's not long until tween time."

Tween time occurred between the last drop of daylight as the sun set and the first bit of darkness, often called First Lavender, which preceded First Black, for it never turned dark all at once. It was at this time that tweener, the largest meal for owls, was served. Coryn and the rest of the Chaw of Chaws — minus Ruby — waited impatiently in Coryn's hollow to find out why Otulissa and Soren had called them to meet so suddenly.

"Where's Ruby?" Otulissa said.

"You know how Ruby hates to get up early," Martin said.

"Can't say I'm loving this myself." Twilight yawned noisily. "Better be good."

Indeed they all seemed rather sleepy, except for Soren and Otulissa.

"Sorry . . . sorry, I'm late," Ruby said, landing in the hollow.

Otulissa looked at Soren. "Do you want to begin?"

Where to begin? Soren thought. Ruby and Martin didn't even know about the Palace of Mists. So first that had to be explained.

Soren began slowly. "There is this place, Ruby and Martin, that we discovered when we were youngsters. It is called the Palace of Mists."

"Palace of Mists," Ruby said with wonder. Soren went on to explain that they had promised Bess they would keep it a secret, except for telling Otulissa. Bess was a scholar and she had agreed to share the library and what she knew with the two most scholarly owls of the Great Tree — Otulissa and the late Ezylryb. Soren then turned to Otulissa. "I think you should tell them about the letter from Bess."

"I committed the letter to memory," she said, "so I will just recite it." Otulissa felt the tension in the hollow mounting, and then she arrived at those astounding three sentences:

"But such is not the case. These star maps were not created by the Others, but by owls. There is in fact a sixth kingdom of owls. It is called the Middle Kingdom, and I believe it is within wing-reach."

One could have heard a feather drop, or a thread of down from a plummel for that matter. There was complete and utter silence. And then everyone started talking at once. "A sixth kingdom?" "So far?" "How do we get there?" "When do we go?" "Do we tell the rest of the tree?" "What do we tell them?"

"Quiet!" Coryn ordered. They all turned to him. "We have to take things in an orderly fashion." Despite his measured tone and careful words, they all could see that Coryn was as excited as they were. He had never been to the Palace of Mists. He had heard about it from the Band and longed to go there and meet the mysterious Bess. And now perhaps to travel to this sixth kingdom — but who would be in charge of the tree? The last time they had left, near disaster had ensued. "Right now, it's not so much a question of when we leave, but how."

Ruby blinked and thought, *How? Fly! How else?*

"Do we tell the parliament right now?" Coryn asked.

Digger stepped forward. "First, I think we have to go to the Palace of Mists. Second, we must review the fragments and discuss all this with Bess. Finally, if indeed we decide to go on and seek the sixth kingdom across the Unnamed Sea — which in itself is a staggering thought — I think someone must know where we have gone. We also must tell that someone of Bess and the Palace of Mists — in case we do not return within one moon cycle."

Soren interjected, "If we do not return within a moon's cycle, there should be arrangements to send a contingent to the Palace of Mists." He paused. "And I think Eglantine would be a good choice. Eglantine along with Primrose. I will speak with them about it."

"All right, I think we've got the beginning of a plan. Tweener will be soon," Coryn said. "I know we're all very excited but, please, not a word about this in the dining hollow. No one must know anything yet."

"Yes, Coryn is right." Soren nodded solemnly. "Not a word to anyone."

CHAPTER THREE

Mrs. Plithiver Perceives

For some, however, words did not have to be spoken. Despite the reputation of reptiles as dull-witted, less evolved, primitive creatures, it was well known that the blind nest-maid snakes of the Great Ga'Hoole Tree — indeed blind snakes serving anywhere as domestic servants in the hollows of owls — had superb sensibilities. It was as if with the loss of their sight, the other senses of these snakes had been honed like the edge of a blade to an extraordinary keenness. Mrs. Plithiver, the nest-maid snake who had served Soren since his hatching, was no exception. Of all the nest-maid snakes in the tree, she perhaps had the most finely tuned sensibilities.

A pale lavender light began to suffuse the dining hall, and as the nest-maid snakes slithered in with the tweener food on their backs — the nut cups of milkberry tea and boneless roasted late-winter mice stuffed with dried caterpillars — Mrs. Plithiver immediately sensed an agitation among the Band, indeed the entire Chaw of Chaws, as they had gathered around her. She served at the table for the Chaw of Chaws, and she knew that something was up. She tensed the muscles behind the slight depressions where her eyes would have been and she began to get glimmerings. The muscles that sheathed the stem glands of nest-maid snakes were the source of the snakes' delicate perceptions, according to Otulissa, who had studied the physiology of blind snakes. She had even written a treatise objecting to the lumping together of blind snakes with other reptiles, who were so often characterized as being animals with "primitive systems."

Even before the owls gathered around her, Mrs. P. had a very clear sense that they had once again received a message of some sort from *that place*, as she thought of it. She could almost smell it. She remembered the first time the Band had come back from it, when they were youngsters: the damp mossy smell, and the mineral tang of stone — stone that never dried or felt the heat of the sun. Over the years, the Band had made many furtive visits and when they returned there was always this wet-moss scent mixed with ever-wet stone. Then, just the day before, when she had gone into Otulissa's hollow, she detected the same smell despite the rather robust fire in Otulissa's grate. Something had come from *that place* — a letter perhaps. Or maybe a visitor had just been there. No matter, the scent lingered on.

There were, of course, many strange places within the kingdoms of owls, ranging from the volcanic lands of Beyond the Beyond to the glaciers of the Northern Kingdoms. But this place was of neither ice nor of fire. It seemed to Mrs. P. that there was something more telling than a mere scent. There was a feeling, like relic vibrations of a deep thrumming, which still reverberated when she had entered Otulissa's hollow that day with some milkberry tea. And *that place* seemed to have a tinge about it, a tincture of something she didn't know or quite understand. Could it be something to do with the Others? Was it somehow akin to the vague Other-ish tingle she felt around the oddments that Trader Mags brought to the tree? Mrs. Plithiver, completely absorbed in her own thoughts, was paying very little attention to the silly blather at the table, which she had decided early on was a cover for what these owls really wanted to talk about. It was this unspoken conversation that was the source of a new agitation, an intense excitement that she sensed among the owls. It was so obvious they had something else on their minds.

"Fancy. Cook's getting too fancy," Twilight was saying.

"Stuffed mouse? Why does a mouse have to be stuffed, and the bones served on the side with this honey dipping sauce?"

"Yeah, I agree," said Digger. "Imagine what Ezylryb would say about this fancy fare."

"Oh, he wouldn't permit it," Otulissa replied. "We always had to eat our meat raw on the night of weather-interpretation or colliering flights."

"What do you mean, 'had to'?" Soren protested. "*I* still insist on it." Soren was now the leader of both the colliering chaw and the weather-interpretation chaw.

"Well, we better get back to raw mice if we're going to go to this —" Twilight started and stopped suddenly.

Otulissa delivered a swift kick to the Great Gray's foot. "You are so indiscreet," she hissed.

"Indiscreet is my middle name," Twilight replied blithely.

It was the vibrations from the kick that set off sparks that burst like a supernova throughout Mrs. P.'s so-called primitive reptilian system. *I've got it!*

"I want to go, Soren," Mrs. P. said in her direct manner.

Soren was simply stupefied. Mrs. P. was suspended from the empty perch usually occupied by the three B's.

"I've known about that place for a long time," she went on.

For a split second he was not sure what place she was referring to.

"That place with the damp moss and the ever-wet stone and the thrumming roar of . . . of water, and I think mist. The mist that clings to your feathers when you come back. The mist that carries the mossy smell."

Soren shook his head in disbelief. "You know all this — but how, Mrs. P.?"

"Soren." She slithered off the perch and wound herself up into a neat coil on the floor of his hollow. She cocked her head and regarded him. It was as if those sightless dents bore directly into his own eyes. "Really, Soren. You know better than to ask how or why. I was with your family before you hatched, and I've been with you ever since — except for that unfortunate time." The "unfortunate time" was when Soren, a mere pre-fledged hatchling, had been captured by a St. Aggie's gang that roamed the forest skies searching for owl chicks who had fallen from their nests. Of course, in Soren's case, he had been shoved out of the nest by his older brother, Kludd. She always referred to Soren's capture and imprisonment in St. Aegolius Academy for Orphaned Owls as "that unfortunate time." Mrs. P. was given to understatement.

Soren coughed slightly. "Yes, foolish of me."

"Not foolish, Soren. You just don't want me to go."

"No, no. You know I have no trouble flying with you. Nearly every member of the Chaw of Chaws has transported you at one time or another."

"Then what is it?" Mrs. P. persisted.

"Well, what would be the point of your coming?"

Let's see . . . Mrs. P. thought. *How to say this diplomatically?* "Well, Soren. I think if I could accompany you to this place of the mists —"

"It's called Palace of Mists, but close enough," Soren said, astonishment just on the edge of his voice. *How in the world does she figure this stuff out?*

"Yes, Palace of Mists. I think I might be able to help you understand these fragments of documents." Soren's beak hung open in amazement. There was no use trying to disguise his wonder now.

Mrs. P. continued. "You know, get a feel for what this new kingdom, this distant land is. What *do* you call it?"

"You know about the sixth kingdom, too?"

"Oh, yes, dear. The whole thing came together for me when Otulissa kicked Twilight at tweener. The vibrations were quite overpowering. I thought I might collapse. Although it's hard for a snake to collapse. You know that offensive expression 'lower than a snake'?" Soren merely blinked. "You see, Soren, if you do decide to go on to this sixth kingdom, after you visit the Palace of Mists . . ."

"You mean you don't know what we've decided?" he said with mock wonder.

"Now Soren, don't get sarcastic with me. It does not become you at all."

"Sorry," he replied, immediately contrite.

"As I was saying, I thought that if you go to this Palace of Mists place and then on to . . ."

"And then on to what?" Soren blinked.

"Well, I don't quite know what to call it. 'Sixth kingdom' doesn't seem to be a proper name, really." The space between the indentations for her eyes furrowed. "It's rather nameless, I suppose, like the Unnamed Sea." She gasped. "Oh dear. That's it. The Unnamed Sea — you want to cross it!!!"

"Mrs. Plithiver." Soren shook his head in wonder. "You are incredible."

"No, no, not at all. I just want to go with you, accompany you, and . . ." She hesitated and then waggled her head slightly as if considering her next thought before she spoke it aloud. "I think, Soren, I might be of help. I mean, this could be a new world for you. If there are owls, they are going to be different owls, with different sensibilities. . . ." She let the last word linger as she stretched herself up. Then, slinging herself over a lower perch, she let herself hang in a configuration that seemed halfway between a question mark and an exclamation point. Mrs. P. was a subtle manipulator of punctuation — bodily punctuation — in service to her discourse.

Soren knew she was absolutely right. She had not exactly called the owls oafish creatures or dunderheads, but she had elegantly made her point about the benefits, the advantages, that her rare sensibilities could confer on this undertaking.

"All right. But I'll have to discuss this with the others first."

"Of course, dear, of course."

"Mrs. P.? You've got to be kidding. Are you yoicks?" Twilight asked.

"She knew all about it?" Otulissa asked, more than dismayed.

"Actually, she said," Soren replied, "that when you kicked Twilight, it all came together for her."

"That'll show you, Otulissa. You shouldn't have kicked me," Twilight muttered.

"I wouldn't have kicked you if you hadn't nearly blurted the whole thing out."

"Quit arguing," Coryn said. Sometimes the Band, who were all older and supposedly more mature than himself, sounded like a bunch of squabbling children. He turned to Digger, the Burrowing Owl. "Digger, I want to hear what you have to say."

Digger shut his eyes for a long time. "Well, there are two parts to this. Will she go with us to the Palace of Mists? And then if we go on, will she accompany us to the Middle Kingdom, as it is called?"

"I don't mind her going to the Palace of Mists, but all the way to the Middle Kingdom?" Gylfie scratched her head with her minuscule talon and began to equivocate. "I mean, it just seems a bit much."

Digger continued. "It's an interesting proposition. Think of it this way, Gylfie: When we fly on an expedition, especially one that involves something unknown or risky, we take you as navigator, Twilight for his fighting skills, and Soren and Otulissa for weather interpretation and coal harvesting. We take our battle claws just in case. In other words, we fly well equipped. We have already decided to include the Chaw of Chaws." He looked at Martin and Ruby. "This was suggested by Bess herself."

"What are you getting at?" Twilight said.

"I am merely saying that Mrs. P. would be a terrific

addition to our — how shall I put it — arsenal? Tool kit? Call it what you may," Digger concluded.

All the owls blinked. This was a peculiar notion. A nest-maid as part of the Chaw of Chaws. But then again, hadn't Mrs. P. flown with the Band long ago when they first came to the Great Ga'Hoole Tree? Hadn't she been the one to perceive the deadly enchantment that the Mirror Lakes in The Beaks could cast on young owls?

"I think it's a very good idea," Coryn said. "I can't tell you what to do. After all, I am . . ." he churred, "merely a king and not an official member of the Chaw of Chaws, but I think we would be foolish to leave Mrs. Plithiver behind for any part of this mission."

And so it was decided the nest-maid snake would accompany them to the Palace of Mists and beyond, if indeed they decided to journey to this sixth kingdom.

CHAPTER FOUR

Chawlets in Training

The chawlets were assembled, but rowdy. Eglantine and Primrose were waiting for them to settle down. The two friends were discussing the revelation from Soren of the Palace of Mists, and the even greater revelation of a sixth owl kingdom. They were pleased that Soren had entrusted them with this information. Eglantine turned and addressed the restless chawlets: "Now, you have all heard of the Chaw of Chaws," Eglantine said as she perched on a limb in front of the young owls who had only been flying for a little more than a moon cycle.

"Of course!" they all cried.

"Our da is in it," Bash, one of Soren and Pelli's triplet daughters, yelled out.

"Yeah, he's a collier," said Blythe.

"But he does weather, too," Bell, the littlest of the three B's, said very seriously.

"Yes, but Soren is not the only owl in the Chaw of Chaws," Eglantine, who was the three B's' aunt, said. "Who

26

can tell me the other members of this distinguished chaw?"

Talons from a half dozen little owls rose in the air. "My auntie almost made it," said one little Pygmy Owl. "My auntie had the yarpie barbies the other night and couldn't go colliering and missed a really good forest fire."

"My auntie's friend got arrested and put in prison during the bad times," said another. Eglantine shot Pelli a frantic glance. She was perched nearby. Eglantine had forgotten how distractible young'uns could be.

Pelli stepped forward. "I have an accomplished aunt, too, but now is not the time for me to tell you about her. This is training time. We have come here to Silverveil, where there has been a small forest fire that we can learn from. Now, who knows what kind of coal this is and where you can find it in the coal beds?" She held up a glowing orange ember pinched between the two front talons of her right foot.

"Orange is my favorite color," Matty, a young Snowy Owl, said.

"Mine's pink," said another. "For my hatchday, Cook says she's going to make me a pink Ga'Hoole nut cake."

"Oh, great Glaux!" Eglantine muttered. "If they start talking about hatchdays . . ."

"Now, young'uns!" Pelli said sharply. "This isn't about favorite colors. It's about coals. All eyes on me, please!"

Finally, the young owlets settled down. They were then divided into three chawlets for evening exercises: ember hunting, weather interpretation, and navigation. Pelli saw to it that the three B's were separated because when they talked and giggled together, they could be quite disruptive. So Blythe was sent with the weather-interpretation chawlet to fly the squally front passing through. Bash was dispatched to some coal beds that still smoldered on the edges of the forest fire, and Bell flew with the navigation chawlet under the direction of Fritha, an up-and-coming young Pygmy Owl who often assisted Gylfie, the navigation chaw's ryb.

"She's not as good as Gylfie," Heggety, a Short-eared Owl, whispered. They were engaged in a very basic exercise of tracing the constellation of the Golden Talons, which had ascended a few nights before and would now be visible through spring and summer and well into autumn.

"I know," Bell replied. "And she's not that much older than we are."

"She's a preenie weenie," said another. Preenie weenie was one of the worst things a young owl could call another.

"Yes, she's always combing Otulissa's primaries," Heggety whispered.

"No whispering, please," Fritha called back. "The best way to learn these configurations is to fly them. Heggety, right behind me now, on my tail. Bell, you fly behind Heggety. Matty, to my port wing, and Max, you to my starboard." Max and Matty had a near midair collision as they became confused about which side was port and which was starboard. "Port here!" Fritha waggled her left wing in an exaggerated manner. "Starboard here." She waggled the other. "I knew this by the time I was your age."

"Oh, go on! Stuck-up Pygmy!" Max muttered.

"No talking now!" Fritha said. "Concentrate. I might give you a pop quiz when we get back to the tree and have you draw the constellations." There was a groan from the four young owls.

"Gylfie never gives pop quizzes!" Bell piped up.

"Gylfie is not here tonight. I am here. I'm the substitute and what I say goes."

"I can't stand substitute rybs," whispered Matty.

The owlets took their positions.

This is so borrrrring! thought Bell. She was a quick learner and knew all the constellations. She could already draw them in her sleep. She wished she had been sent with the weather-interpretation chaw. Maybe this squall would have scuppers with real baggywrinkles. The scuppers were the side trenches of a gale or squall where the edges of the wind spilled over. The baggywrinkles were the shredded air currents that lay just outside the scuppers. Oh, Bell knew all about the structure of a gale or squall, although neither she nor any of these young owls had flown in a true storm yet. Just her luck to miss out on climbing the baggywrinkles, and dancing in the scuppers! Blythe was so lucky!! Tonight would be the night and here she was, stuck with a substitute, missing all the fun.

There was a rowdy old song that the weather-interpretation chaw used to sing when Ezylryb was the ryb. Soren had sung it to them once but Pelli, their mum, got very angry and said it had too many naughty words and wouldn't permit it. But Bell could remember the melody and many of the words, which began to stream through her head now as she followed Heggety.

We are the owls of the weather chaw.
We take it blistering.
We take it all.

Roiling, boiling gusts,
we're the owls with the guts.

For blizzards our gizzards
do tremble with joy.
An ice storm, a gale, how we love blinding hail.
We fly forward and backward
Upside down and flat.
Do we flinch? Do we wail?
Do we skitter or scutter?
No, we yarp one more pellet
and fly straight for the gutter!

There was another verse that she couldn't remember because it was just at that point that her mum had cut her da off. It was something about stinky nights. Bell gave a small start, for at that moment she felt the curling edge of a dampish wind. *Maverick swillage?* she thought. *Spun off from a nearby gale?* The night had suddenly become cloudy. *What's the point of tracing the Golden Talons if you can't even see it?* she wondered. Maybe she'd just fly off for a short look, because if there was a gale with real scuppers . . . Oh, it was just grit in her gizzard that Blythe might dance the hurly-burly in the scuppers, and she'd come back all braggy about it. Bell just had to try it. No one from the navigation chaw would miss her when she was flying double tail so far back. And she'd only be gone a minute . . . or two . . . or three . . . certainly no more than five.

CHAPTER FIVE

The Palace of Mists

I t was strange, Mrs. P. thought. From a great distance, she could hear an enormous sound of the crush of water plummeting, but through that roar she could make out so many other sounds — voices of the Guardians and Bess. She listened beyond these, however, and perceived not echoes but vibrations or perhaps other ripples. Then, within the ripples she sensed — what should she call them? — lumps? Seeds? Yes, seeds from a time long ago when other voices might have stirred the mists of these palace chambers. It was a peculiar place, which seemed composed as much of mist as stone. The palace with its turrets, spires, and towers was tucked behind the great curtain of cascading water, and its back wall was the soaring stone cliff.

"You brought a nest-maid snake? Mrs. Plithiver, you call her?" Bess was whispering, thinking that she could not be heard. But, of course, Mrs. P. could hear every word and so much more. But she didn't feel that it was time for her to say anything — not yet, at least.

"Yes," Soren was saying. "But don't worry." Mrs. P. could feel Bess shrug. "She is very discreet. Nest-maids are, you know."

Not all, Mrs. P. thought. *Not Audrey. Biggest gossip in the tree.*

Bess now turned to Otulissa. "So you explained to them?"

"Well, as best I could," Otulissa replied.

"I have found more document fragments. It's all quite amazing. I'll go fetch them." She flew to the stone stacks toward the rear of the library, a series of deep niches in which scrolls and books were placed. While she was gone, a draft of cold mist swirled down, fogging the table where they perched.

"It's that storm that came up," Twilight said. "A real wester. Odd this time of year. Imagine what a waggle Ezylryb would have gotten out of this one." Like a fleeting shadow, the worrisome thought of the three B's caught in something like this crossed Soren's mind. But they were safe. Pelli and Eglantine and Primrose would have made sure they got to one of the numerous hollows near the training grounds where the chawlets were practicing.

When Bess returned, she carried a botkin stuffed with fragments of old scrolls. She carefully took them out of their oiled mouse-skin covers.

"For all this time," Soren said, "we have known that there was this place that we called The Elsewhere. But never before had we imagined that there was a kingdom of owls there. We thought perhaps it was a place the Others had been, but never owls. Whatever led you to think that there were owls there, Bess?"

She drew out a fragment from one of the botkins. "This was my first clue." She put down the piece of parchment. At first glance, it looked like a small bit that had been torn from one of the star charts because there were constellations sketched on it. Bess took out a magnifying glass from a pouch made of vole skin. This instrument always fascinated the Band. It was a tool of the Others, and Bess used it to read the dim handwriting on the most ancient of manuscripts. She set the glass down on the torn piece of parchment. "Now look. Tell me, what do you see?"

The owls peered over the glass and then all gasped.

"An owl's eye!" Twilight said.

"B-b-b-but . . . but . . ." Otulissa stammered. "That proves nothing. I mean, an Other could have drawn that."

"Yes, possibly," Bess agreed. "Although I feel the pressure used with the writing tool is not that of an Other. It's a fragile line. But if you are not convinced, look at this." She slid the magnifying glass down a bit. It revealed talon writing. There was no doubt about it. And although the foreign words seemed slightly familiar, there was one word that sailed out: *Glaux!*

"It's the same in any language, isn't it?" Gylie said. "Krakish, Hoolian . . . and . . . and . . ."

Bess whispered now. "I have been studying and have just started to understand a few words of the sixth kingdom's language. And this much I know. They are not words of any other creatures but owls." The owls nodded. They believed her. Still, it was staggering. What would these owls be like? What would they think of Hoolian owls? Were they hugely intelligent, far more intelligent than the owls of their own Five Kingdoms? There was a vast sea between the known world of the owls and this Middle Kingdom. So inaccessible was the Middle Kingdom that it might as well be a star in the Golden Talons. And now they were being told that owls were there.

"I think the part that perplexes us all the most," Digger began slowly, contemplating every word, "is that you say we can fly there. That it is within wingreach. It's hard to imagine flying over an ocean as vast as the Unnamed Sea. Did you find islands on the charts? Places we can rest?" he asked.

"No, none at all." Once more she dipped into the botkin with her talon, and took out a fatter scroll. With great care, she unrolled the parchment. It had no writing but just a series of wavy lines. "No islands, just air currents."

"Air currents?" Otulissa said.

"I found this chart quite a while ago. But I had no idea what it meant. Well, that is not quite true. I sensed it could have something to do with wind — airflow and the like — but it was incomprehensible. Not just a puzzle, but a maze. A labyrinth of wind. But some of these might be windkins."

"Windkins! You don't say!" Otulissa said. A windkin was a companion air current for another wind from an opposite quadrant. The two winds worked together in strange but complementary ways. Otulissa peered closer. Her beak was tracing the wavy lines. "Yes, definitely a windkin, and I can tell you exactly where this windkin is."

"You can?" said Soren.

"Yes." Otulissa hopped over to a perch by an immense map of the five known kingdoms of the owl world. "I believe it is a companion to this one." She pointed with a long talon to a remote firth in the Northern Kingdoms. "You see, they fit together like interlocking teeth — if they were together, that is. But they're not. They've split apart. This is the companion windkin to the one on the fragment."

"That's near the Firth of Grundenspyrr!" Soren said. "The home of Theo, the first blacksmith."

"Exactly."

"And if we draw a line to the opposite quadrant we will find that the windkin that Bess has shown us on this fragment is right here." She traced a line across and then her talon stopped at a point on the far northwest coast of Beyond the Beyond. "Look. There is even an inlet here similar in shape to the Firth of Grundenyspyrr right on the edge of the Unnamed Sea."

"But we all have at one time or another flown in that region of the Northern Kingdoms. Why have we missed that windkin all these years?" Gylfie asked.

"It's at a very high altitude," Otulissa explained. "And perhaps when we were there, we experienced some remnant downdrafts, but they would not have seemed all that different from any other downdrafts. I knew about windkins because once, years ago, I decided to do some extra-credit work for Ezylryb in the weather-interpretation chaw and learned about them that way."

The members of the Band exchanged quick glances. *Typical!* they all thought. As a young student in the weather-interpretation chaw, Otulissa was always doing extra-credit work.

"But what does this all mean?" Ruby asked.

"It means that there is a way across the Unnamed Sea," Otulissa said.

"But it's huge! It's so vast, it would take days of flying," Martin said.

"Not with a windkin stream. We'll hardly have to flap a wing, once we find the central stream. You see, the shortest distance between two points, even two very far points, is not always the fastest route. And that is the beauty of a windkin trough. But before you actually find that trough, or center stream, it is sort of like being tossed around in a maze, flying these windkins. It can be very rough. I mean, if there were just a . . . a . . ." Otulissa was searching for a word.

"A key?" Bess said with great excitement.

"Yes, a key," Otulissa replied.

"Then, that is what this must be! I felt it had something to do with these air currents." Bess reached with her talon into the bottom of the botkin. She held up a small fragment of parchment. "This," she said, "unlocks the maze — a maze of wind far above the vast sea that must be crossed."

"You mean, if we use this we can find our way through the windkin to the trough or the central stream, or whatever you call it?" Gylfie asked. The tiny Elf Owl had hopped onto Twilight's shoulder to get a better look at the fragment of paper Bess had just set down.

"It will help you. You see, there is an equal sign by these symbols and then a little section of wavy lines. And here, when you look at the larger fragment, you can see that some of these symbols have been dropped into the pattern of wavy lines every once in a while. I think they are a sort of key to the direction of the wind currents, but I'm not sure I quite understand the symbols."

"Great Glaux!" Soren and Otulissa both blurted out.

"What is it?" Bess asked. "Do you understand the key?"

"These are standard . . . well, almost standard weather, wind, and temperature symbols that we all use in weather interpretation," Soren replied.

"*Almost* standard?" Twilight said, and took a perch above Soren and Otulissa.

"Yes," Otulissa answered. "Almost. These look like a very ancient form of the symbols we know. That triangle with the little tail on top — well, the tail is different, but it means rising temperature in this part of the air currents."

"And those sort of mountainy-looking things," Martin said, "that means thermal upswing, which is different from a regular updraft — more gradual, not so sudden."

"Look at that!" Ruby gasped. "It's a bird skull. A tumblebones!" Ruby was also a member of the weather-interpretation chaw, and this symbol had remained the same for years. The rim of a hurricane's eye was sometimes called a tumblebones. If a bird was caught in a tumblebones, it spun around and around until it died. It was said that even its bones could never escape.

"But this isn't a hurricane we're looking at here," Twilight said.

"Not cyclical winds." Otulissa had become quite thoughtful as she peered down, studying the wavy lines and then glancing between them and the key. "These are basically high, fast, thermal drafts. They flow contrary to the weather vectors that we are familiar with. But you see this key really applies to the edges. The wind-kins, including the tumblebones, are the crisscrossing drafts that one has to climb through to get to the central trough. Imagine a ladder of wind — or even a very violent baggywrinkle — that we would climb at the edges of a gale, but much more dangerous. The windkins brace the central stream, more or less. Think of them as eddies that swirl off the central current of a river. They can be very confused, tumultuous, rotating in opposite directions. To cross them in order to enter the stream and to get out at the end — that is the hard part. But the key will help." Otulissa hesitated. "I see only one problem."

Bess blinked and wilfed a bit. Mrs. P. sensed that Bess saw the problem, too, and Mrs. P. had a glimmer of what that problem might be.

"Yes?" Soren said.

"What's the problem?" Gylfie asked.

"How do we get back? Does the current go in reverse? And the key, does it apply to just going one way or can we somehow return using the same key? Perhaps there are differences coming back and it won't work," Otulissa said. "Can we reverse it?"

They could all see Bess hesitate. "Not exactly reverse it. And I have tried to do some inverse mathematics relating to standard air currents . . ."

"Yes, I can see that might be helpful, but what if we tried a quadratic differential to the fifth power?" Otulissa said.

"I'm lost," Soren muttered.

"Oh, I understand completely," Twilight snorted.

"Perhaps," Digger said in his slow, thoughtful way, "we need not resort to mathematics at all."

"And why not?" Gylfie exclaimed.

"Well," Digger continued, "what I am thinking is that we are just now learning about this sixth kingdom. But *they* apparently have known about *us* for a long time. How these fragments got here is anyone's guess. But they got here, and this means some owl, some emissary from the sixth kingdom, came here at some time in history. Therefore, can we not conclude that if they came here there is a way back, a way from *there* to *here?*"

The owls looked at Digger, stunned by the lovely simplicity of his notion.

Soren turned to Coryn. "All right. So we'll go?" Coryn nodded.

Mrs. Plithiver now coughed delicately. "There is one thing I would like to suggest, Coryn."

"What is that, Mrs. P.?" Coryn had a profound respect for Mrs. P. He had secretly been thrilled when Soren had raised the question of her coming with them.

"I think we should leave the battle claws behind."

"What?" Twilight yelped. "You can't be serious!"

"I am perfectly serious," Mrs. P. said. She had coiled up taller and swiveled her head toward Twilight. "I just have a feeling that we should not bring them. I have a sense about these owls. We shall look very poor to them if we arrive rattling battle claws. As Digger said, we can conclude that they came here sometime in the past. They flew among us, observed us. No one, apparently, knew they were here. If they had arrived armed to the beak, someone would have noticed. And I, for one, would have thought it very bad form."

"I think Mrs. P. is right," Soren said. "I can remember one of Ezylryb's finest speeches, in which he said that although boldness of action is always called for, it must be tempered by wisdom and restraint, and too often it is not. And that we had nothing to fear except fear itself."

Coryn blinked and his eyes blazed. "Fear itself! It is a terrible thing. You are absolutely right." He nodded at Soren and then Mrs. Plithiver. "During that horrid time of the Golden Tree when the milkberries never changed their color and those owls became fixated on the ember, they were seized with superstition about the ember's powers. Superstition is closely linked to fear. It was that, I feel, not respect for the ember that led them to build a prison. Owls were systematically deprived of their rights, their dignity. Otulissa was locked up, and then Madame Plonk, and then Primrose! What could have been more contrary to the entire meaning of the great tree?" Never had the owls seen Coryn as passionate. "Mrs. Plithiver is absolutely right. We must leave our weapons behind. We must come in peace. This is my command as monarch of the tree."

Coryn rarely issued absolute commands. The owls were silent for several seconds. Even Twilight did not raise a protest but appeared impressed by the force of Coryn's argument. The construction of a barred hollow and the imprisonment of owls had been, of all the bad things that happened during those awful days of the Golden Tree, the most shocking violation to the code and the honor of the Guardians of Ga'Hoole. There was no one who could look back without shame on those terrible moon cycles when the great tree had appeared to flourish, but the gizzards of some of its owls had hardened and withered.

"Now," Coryn continued, "there are other practical matters to think about. If we do successfully negotiate these windkins and find the current of streaming air, how long will it take us? And if not weapons, what should we take — food? Can we eat on the wing?"

Otulissa had been looking hard at Bess, but now turned to address Coryn. "There are two sun symbols on the key and only two newing moon symbols, one slightly more shaded. I would think that means that the flight is a day, a night, another day, and part of another night, for the shading of the moon has barely increased on the second night."

"That's so short!" Gylfie gasped in astonishment.

"About the same time as flying from the great tree to the northernmost reaches of the Northern Kingdoms," Otulissa said.

"But still, there's no place to stop in between. No islands. No Ice Narrows with cliffs," Martin whispered.

"Yes, but if this stream is what I think it is, we'll barely burn any energy getting there."

"It seems amazing that no one has discovered this before now," Ruby wondered aloud.

"Well, as I said, it's high-altitude flying, and you have to negotiate these wind ladders and the dangers of the tumblebones," Otulissa replied.

"So, are you saying we don't need to take much?" Soren asked. "What about this key? Should we bring it? We will probably need it."

"I don't think we need that much. Except perhaps time, right now. Time to study more. This key is not hard to memorize. I think we should all try to commit at least a piece of it to memory. I will try to memorize all of it."

"What about gifts?" Gylfie said. "If we brought something, you know, a present, it might show that we come in good faith and good gizzard."

"That's a lovely idea, Gylfie," Mrs. P. said. "But whatever could we bring?"

"Maybe something simple," Soren said. "There is a lot of rabbit's ear moss that grows in the Shadow Forest. It's the best moss in the whole world for lining a young'un's bed. I always bring some back for Pelli and the chicks. Maybe it doesn't grow in the sixth kingdom."

"Brilliant!" Bess exclaimed. "Yes, I think that would be just the thing. Much better than those geegaws you tell me Trader Mags is always dragging around."

"Absolutely!" Otulissa nodded firmly in approval. She then swiveled her head toward Bess. She blinked her eyes shut for several long seconds. "Bess, your revelations this evening . . ."

"Oh, do not call them revelations, Otulissa," Bess protested. "That sounds so . . . so emotional. I prefer to think of them as evidence. These are documents, dare I say primary source documents, that you can hold in your talons. You can see that these are the writings of owls."

"Yes, yes, of course." Otulissa nodded in great deference. She had understood for a long time that Bess was a scholar equal to herself. "I just mean to say, if I may put it plainly . . ."

"Oh, please do."

"Bess, this is simple. It would be helpful, since you understand this language, or at least many of the words beyond the one that we share in common — Glaux — that you would come with us."

They all looked at Bess expectantly. The slender Boreal Owl wilfed, suddenly growing much slimmer. "No . . . no. I don't leave the Palace of Mists. Ever!"

"Never?" Martin asked in wonder.

"Never," Bess repeated.

It was decided that the Chaw of Chaws would stay on for several more days at the Palace of Mists. They would study the charts of the windkins, memorize the key, and Otulissa and Bess would embark on an intense study of the random fragments of the peculiar language they had found on the documents.

Soren reminded them that he had charged Primrose and Eglantine with the duty of informing the Parliament of their mission.

"And if we do not return? If Eglantine and Primrose go to search for us and they do not return?" Digger asked.

All of the owls turned their heads slowly toward Coryn. "The search will be given up. They cannot risk the entire great tree and its Guardians for this . . . this venture."

"But can we risk our king?" Gylfie asked quietly.

"Kings are replaceable — but all of the Guardians of the great tree?" He paused. "Never!"

CHAPTER SIX

Where's Bell?

The dozen young owls and their rybs were huddled in the large many-chambered hollow of an immense beech tree. Pelli perched on the edge of the hollow looking out into the buffeting winds. All the owls were back except for the navigation chawlet led by Fritha. Pelli hoped it hadn't been a mistake to send them out with such a young owl. Fritha was clever, though still young in her judgment. But who would have expected these squall lines that had come bashing through! There had been only one to begin with — no sign of an entire line of them one after the other. Pelli hoped against hope they were not a prelude to westers. But that was a definite possibility.

"I see them!" Eglantine cried out from a branch she was perched on outside the tree.

"They're coming, Mum," Bash said.

"Don't worry, Mum. Bell is fine, I'm sure." Blythe tucked in beneath her mum's wing and gave her a snuggle.

"Yes, Bell will be here soon," Bash said, and squeezed between the feather trousers of her mum's legs. Both owlets were trying to be very brave, but they had never seen their mum this worried. They could feel her heart pumping and a terrible grinding in her gizzard even though they had not eaten for a while, so there were no bones in there.

Pelli blinked, then wiped her eyes clear twice with the third eyelid that owls use often in foul weather. The figures melted out of the darkness. There should be five, including Fritha. She spotted Fritha flying the point position, and there was Max to port and Matty to starboard as well as Heggety. *Surely she is not having anyone fly double tail in this weather*, Pelli thought, and felt her gizzard seize, then give an anguishing wrench. "Bell! Where's Bell?" she shreed in the high-pitched cry of a Barn Owl, as Fritha landed on a wildly tossing branch of the beech tree. The young Pygmy Owl gasped and gave an anguished cry.

"She was right behind Heggety! And Heggety was right behind me, and then suddenly she was gone!" Fritha could barely speak coherently through the sobs that wracked her body. "I don't know what happened. It was *before* the weather turned so bad. She just vanished." The young Pygmy Owl was hiccuping and sobbing so much her words were hardly understandable.

"Calm down!" Eglantine ordered. Blythe and Bash were wailing and clutching their mum, burying themselves in her belly feathers.

"When did you notice she was gone?" Primrose demanded.

"Uh . . . uh . . ." Fritha hesitated.

"What were your bearings?" Silence.

Eglantine stepped up to the quivering Pygmy Owl who had wilfed to half her normal size. "Fritha, you are the best of Gylfie's navigation students. You must know your bearings."

"I think we were about three points east of Declan." Declan was the third star in the third rear toe on the starboard side of the Golden Talons.

"And what was your position north or south?" Eglantine pressed.

"Maybe four points south of Triga." Triga was a star in a front toe on the same side of the Golden Talons.

"I'm going out to search," Pelli announced.

"You will do no such thing." Eglantine planted herself in front of Pelli. "Primrose and I know how to conduct a search in this kind of weather. Your place is here with your chicks."

"Stay, Mum, stay! Don't leave us!" Blythe and Bash cried.

"Yes," said Pelli quietly. "Yes, you are right."

"Now, don't worry," Primrose said. "We'll find her. Remember, Eglantine and I wound up being double chawed, in search-and-rescue and tracking. That was Ezylryb's idea, shortly before he died. So we both know the crucial wind patterns when the squalls come in from this direction. We're well trained for this situation, Pelli."

Pelli closed her eyes. *Situation! How has my darling Bell become a situation? How do I tell Soren?* She cut off the thought almost immediately.

There had been scuppers and baggywrinkles in this gale. One minute, Bell had been dancing — doing the hurly-burly, in fact, the very dance that she had always heard the weather-interpretation chaw owls gabbling about — and then something happened. It was as if the central trough of the gale collapsed. The scuppers fell through and she with them. Her gizzard turned to stone, and she felt like it was dropping out of her, but then suddenly there was a warm draft and she had been sucked straight up. She bounced mercilessly at the top of this strange warm air. It was useless to try to fly, but Bell felt herself blown relentlessly in one direction. Was this a hurricane? Shouldn't be, at this time of year. But maybe it was. All the horrible stories of owls caught in the rim of a hurricane's eye, never escaping, sent agonizing surges through Bell's gizzard. Suddenly, from nowhere, she felt a powerful whack on the back of her head. That was almost the last thing she remembered. Then she was spinning, and then there was nothing.

CHAPTER SEVEN

The Tomorrow Line

The Chaw of Chaws had never been this far west in the Beyond as they headed to the remote inlet of the Unnamed Sea, where they believed they would find the source of a windkin. They hoped this windkin, if they could negotiate it, would ultimately lead to the high stream of wind that would carry them to the sixth kingdom. An undeniable tension now seized the eight owls. They chatted nervously of everything but that which they feared most — the unknown that lay ahead, and the loss of the familiar world they were leaving behind, perhaps never to see again.

"Say that word once more, Otulissa," Martin asked.

"Jouzho."

"And it means 'Middle Kingdom'?" Twilight, who had never had any interest in any foreign language, suddenly seemed fascinated by Jouzhen, the language of the sixth kingdom.

"Not exactly. 'Jouzho' means 'middle,' and then when

you add the suffix 'kyn,' it means Middle Kingdom. Together, Jouzhenkyn." Otulissa, of course, had gotten her talons on every scrap that had anything to do with the language of the Middle Kingdom. She had kept Bess up often until well past midday with her questions, and together they had compiled a dictionary of sorts. If anyone could learn a language fast, it was Otulissa. Years before, she had almost mastered Krakish by the time of their first journey to the Northern Kingdoms. "It's not a phonetic language exactly," she said.

"How can you tell, if you've never heard it spoken?" Digger asked.

"Well, I just sense it. You know, when you've done as much language study as I have you get a feel for these things." The sound of Otulissa's voice dwindled off in the increasingly turbulent air, and silence now fell upon the owls. There were thick swirls of fog obscuring the moon, the stars, and even the land below. *We might never see what we are leaving,* Soren thought, and felt a small twist in his gizzard.

Ruby broke the silence. "What's that way ahead?" A sudden wind had cleared off the blanketing fog and, beneath the starlight and the shine of the moon glinting in the distance, there was a silken expanse of darkness.

"That which lies between us and Jouzhenkyn: that is, the Unnamed Sea," Otulissa spoke softly.

All the owls felt tremors pass through their gizzards. As the sea drew closer, they felt they had to keep their gaze even steadier on the land. Just offshore, not more than a quarter of a league from the breaking waves, was a rock that spiked from the water like a wolf's fang.

Finally, Digger, who as a Burrowing Owl probably had the closest association with things of earth and of soil, spoke up. "I think we should light down on that rock before we start flying over this ocean. You know, a sort of . . ." His voice faded.

But they all knew what he meant. A last good-bye. A farewell to the known — to rocks, to trees, although there were precious few of those in the Beyond. Yes, good-bye to all that they had known and held dear. What would these owls of the Middle Kingdom be like? Were there species they had never seen? What would they eat? Were there voles in the Middle Kingdom? These were all questions they had discussed at one time or another since they had found out about the sixth kingdom. But there were other questions and thoughts left unspoken. Soren in particular was racked with doubts and — yes — fears. Was it reckless of him to go off, to leave Pelli and the three B's? Soren swiveled his head to watch a cloud that had been stretched by the wind into a shape that looked like a leaping fish. *Sky fish!* It had been a game when they were younger to chase such clouds. They had called it sky fishing. He noticed that the rest of the owls were swiveling their heads this way and that. They were not looking just at the sky fish but, like himself, they were all scanning the air they flew through, drinking in with their eyes the things they loved, the things that defined their world. The clouds, the wind, the way the moonlight fell through the night haze — all these elements of the sky.

As they roosted on the off-lying rock, they took from their botkins the strengthening mixture that Bess had made for them. She had told them it would ensure that they could fly "forever." She had then churred softly and added, "Well, maybe not forever, but long enough for you to find your way through the windkins and into the stream."

Otulissa turned, putting her tail toward the sea. "There's the inlet over there," she said, nodding toward land. "You can't tell from here, but it looks so much like the one in the Firth of Grundenspyrr."

"How high do we have to fly," Martin asked, "until we meet up with these windkins?"

"Not just how high, but how far out," Otulissa said. "So far, there have been no remnant downdrafts to give us any clues, as there were in the Northern Kingdoms.

Flying at that high an altitude for a long time is going to tire us out too quickly."

"So, in other words," Soren said, "we'll have to keep alert for even the slightest downdrafts, and then we go up?"

"Exactly. And that is when the key will really help us. It will be like a guide to climb our way through it. In the meantime, I think we should make the most of the light air right now." Otulissa paused and turned to Gylfie. "Gylfie, the windkin will be oriented in the same direction as the mouth of the inlet. So what should our course be?"

Gylfie swiveled her head toward the inlet and began to take a bearing on the angle, then flipped her head back and up until it appeared to be completely turned around on her small shoulders and pointed straight up. "Well, we should be following a course two points off the western paw of the Big Raccoon," Gylfie said somewhat tentatively.

And rightfully so, Mrs. Plithiver thought as she considered the hesitancy in Gylfie's voice. She had settled herself in a neat coil just behind Soren's neck and between his shoulders, in what she thought of as her transport coil, which was tighter and more compact than her sleeping coil. Where they were heading might constitute a maze of crosscurrents, and Mrs. P. sensed that the old navigation strategies were not going to work at all. She had a feeling that it was going to be more luck and intuition than anything else.

Nonetheless, they set off on the course that Gylfie, known for her extraordinary navigational abilities, had set. As they flew, the smooth night air seemed an eerie prelude, a deceptive lead-in to what lay ahead.

"First downdraft! I think I felt it! Subtle, but there," Otulissa's voice swelled with confidence.

"Can we go up yet?" Martin asked.

"Not quite. We need to find more turbulence before we start up."

Mrs. Plithiver knew, in the peculiar way that she knew many things, that the owls' gizzards had been emboldened with this announcement. She felt Soren thrust forward in flight with a renewed energy.

But as the minutes elapsed and the moon began its descent and another downdraft had yet to be detected, Mrs. Plithiver felt that confidence ebbing away. In relay teams of two, Otulissa and the others had flown out in radiating circles to locate another downdraft, but there was none to be found. They were in the darkest part of the night, normally a comforting time for owls, but now they knew that in a few more hours the night sky would become threadbare, the black leaking from it. At a time when they usually would be returning to their hollows, here there was only the vast sea — no land, no trees, nothing. And worse than that, the sun would be rising behind them — a scalding sun, for the reflections would unroll ahead of them on the sea — and their eyes would blister in its uncompromising light.

Mrs. Plithiver suddenly coiled tighter. "What is it, Mrs. P.?" Soren asked.

"There's something below, Soren." The clouds were so thick at that moment it was hard to see what she was talking about. "It feels familiar. I think . . . I think . . ." She didn't want to say it, but she knew that below them the wolf's fang rock broke through the water. They were back to the exact same place they had been the previous night!

A few seconds later, the clouds cleared off. A collective groan reverberated through the small company of owls and, exhausted, they began to circle in steep banking turns.

Twilight landed first on the rock. "We're back . . . back where we started from," he said with great disgust.

They were all silent. This rock had been the scene of their last good-byes to all the things they had treasured and now that they were back, it made those farewells seem false and those things that they treasured a bit tarnished.

"What happened to that windkin?" Ruby moaned.

"I say we just fly straight up and grab it," Twilight boomed. "Flying straight out and looking for the odd downdraft didn't get us anywhere, and look at all the energy we burned doing that."

"At high altitudes you burn energy much faster. It's a fact, Twilight, and I don't care how strong a flier you are," Otulissa snapped.

"Well, a fat lot of good your way is doing us. We're just flying around in circles," Twilight sneered.

"I agree with Twilight," Ruby said.

"Stop bickering, the lot of you!" Mrs. P. reprimanded. "You'd think you were a bunch of chicks out on your first chaw practice."

"But what about the key?" Gylfie said in a whiny voice. "It's supposed to work. Did you use it to gauge the temperature changes, Otulissa?"

"There were no temperature changes." Otulissa looked almost mournfully at the temperascope, a clever device that Ezylryb himself had invented for measuring changes in temperature. "The gauge never changed. Never went up, never went down. So the key was useless." She sighed.

"A key only works if you put it in the right slot," Mrs. Plithiver said.

"It's not that kind of key, really, Mrs. P.," Soren said. "And if it were, we obviously haven't found the right slot." Soren felt Mrs. P. give a slight shiver. It was a shiver of disapproval at his tone. She would not scold him out loud when they were with others, but she had ways of communicating her disapproval silently.

"Well, how do we find the right slot?" Otulissa asked.

"You're overthinking the problem," Mrs. P. said. "Use the key as a key."

"Now, what does that mean?" Twilight asked.

She did not reply to the Great Gray, but swung her head and skewered Gylfie, the navigator, with her blind eyes. "Gylfie, you are navigating as you normally would, by flying four points off the western paw of the whatever raccoon, this way or that way off the Golden Talons, taking into consideration the wind strength and direction and so on and so on. I don't think that will work. These constellations are slipping away. I can feel it as we approach the curve. I even feel something is happening to time as we approach the . . ." Mrs. P. waggled her head high into the air as if searching for the right word. "The tomorrow line!" she said suddenly.

"The tomorrow line?" they all echoed.

"You see, this is not like when you go on a night flight

and fly from midnight into the next morning. For you owls, that time is continuous — at least in the world that you know. The new night — the tomorrow — begins the next evening at First Black. But I think we have to think differently about where we are flying. In a funny way, I feel that as we continue to fly across this sea, somehow time is behaving differently. Maybe it is the influence of this central stream of fast-moving air. I'm not sure, but look: We know the Earth is round. If it is night here, it must be day someplace else. We know this from the movement of the stars, from our movement around the sun. We cannot always live in a world capped by the night. So we know that tomorrow must start somewhere. That place is out there. How many leagues? I don't know. But that's where tomorrow begins."

"I think we'll know it when we get there. It will be like a hole in the wind — no wind," Mrs. P. said.

Gylfie blinked. She had a logical mind, the mind of a navigator. She was used to plotting courses using the angle of the stars and the most favorable wind directions. It was mathematical, and although time was involved it was not the kind of time Mrs. P. was talking about. Of this she was sure. But at this point there were few other options.

Coryn had been silent throughout this entire discussion. He now turned to Gylfie. "Gylfie, you have served admirably as navigator, but what if what Mrs. P. is saying is true?"

"You are absolutely right," Gylfie said. "This is not my kind of navigation. Soren should fly with Mrs. P. in my usual spot."

"Good." Coryn nodded. "I say, after we have rested a bit, we should fly to tomorrow."

"Pardon me, sir." Mrs. P. could not bring herself to address the king simply as "Coryn." "But I think if we are not too tired, we should go as quickly as possible. The point is to fly as fast as we can away from the dawn toward this new world."

The eight owls blinked rapidly in confusion. They looked at the horizon.

Digger spoke first in his ponderous voice. "What Mrs. P. suggests is that we are right now trapped between the here and now and tomorrow. To break out of this trap, we must fly fast toward the tomorrow line."

"And you say we'll know it when we get there?" Soren flipped his head straight up and twisted it around so he could speak directly to Mrs. P.

"Oh, you'll know it, Soren, don't worry. You'll know it when you get there."

So as the dawn broke, casting a soft pink sheen across the unusually calm waters of the sea, the eight owls lifted from the wolf's fang rock. On the distant horizon, low clouds were strung like pearls on a strand. *The strand of tomorrow?* Soren wondered.

CHAPTER EIGHT

Blue in the Night

Something blue, like fog at tween time, hovered over
Bell. She blinked, and blinked again, then squinted. A
form came into focus. "Matron?" Bell asked. It was a sen-
sible question, for it was the matron who organized the
nursing and care of wounded owls. And Bell knew she
was a wounded owl. Every bone, every feather seemed
to ache.

"Matron?" the voice echoed. The accent was strange.
Bell was suddenly very frightened.

"Where am I? What has happened?" *Is this even an owl?*
she thought as the creature bent over her. "W-w-wh ...
w-what," she stammered. "What are you?" It was a bird. It
even looked like an owl — perhaps a Snowy, but there
were certain things about its features that reminded Bell
of a Spotted Owl. Yes, something definitely spotted, but
then ... and this was the most incredible thing of all —
Spotted or Snowy — this owl was blue! Its feathers were
the color of a faded day sky. "What are you?" Bell repeated.

"Striga," the blue owl said.

"Striga?" Bell repeated. "It sounds . . . sounds Krakish."

The owl's eyes, a very pale yellow, were suddenly alert. A riffle went through its feathers. "I come from a faraway place," the owl replied in halting words.

Bell blinked. Her dark eyes shone brightly. "Of course. You must come from the Northern Kingdoms, where they speak Krakish. There are many Snowy Owls there. You must be one of them . . . a . . . a blue one. And . . . and you must be a Glauxian Brother . . . on a pilgrimage, right?" she finished weakly. This outburst had sapped Bell's energy, which was very low.

"Yes . . . yes . . . a pilgrimage from a faraway place, a very faraway place."

"And your name is Striga and you'll take care of me?" Bell whispered.

"Yes, Striga . . . I am the Striga." The blue owl felt something course through him that was almost beyond happiness, a rapturous exaltation. *I must help this little one,* he thought. *I must help her.*

As soon as the weather cleared, Pelli flew with the chawlets as fast as she could back to the Great Ga'Hoole Tree. Eglantine and Primrose had remained behind to continue the search for Bell. Pelli had wanted to stay, but knew they were right in insisting that she return to the great tree and send back Doc Finebeak, the renowned retired tracker, who had recently settled there.

Fly! Fly! Pelli commanded herself. *Think of nothing but getting back to the great tree.* Surely Doc Finebeak wouldn't say no to her urgent request. He had retired, he was older, and perhaps his tracking senses were not as keen as they used to be, but he couldn't refuse her. She was absolutely gizzard-sick. Every time she thought of tiny Bell, a ghastly squishiness seized her gizzard. From a distance, she caught the first glimpses of the great tree, and at that same moment a strong headwind blew up. It felt as if she were slamming into a wall.

"Fly two points off the wind!" she called out to the chawlets. For truly, they could not fly a straight course but would have to tack, slicing back and forth at an angle to this headwind to gain any kind of forward movement. Hours would be added on to their journey, but there was nothing else to do.

Meanwhile, back in the great tree, Doc Finebeak was peering out of the hollow he shared with Madame Plonk. "Strange weather we're having. First those westers, and now this contrary wind swooping down from the Northern Kingdoms. Yes, it's got a bite to it, all right." He had been studying the weather fronts for the better part of the early evening and turned now toward Madame Plonk. "I say, my dear. What's that spider doing on your head?"

Octavia, their nest-maid snake, giggled to herself as she prepared some milkberry tea.

"Spider?" Madame Plonk replied. "What are you talking about, Docky? It's not a spider. It's a black velvet hat, a *chapeau*, Trader Mags calls it."

"Oh . . . er . . . umm . . . well, it's quite fetching, Plonkie. Yes, the black velvet" — *whatever that is*, he thought — "against your white feathers. Lovely. Ah, here comes Octavia with tea in the coronation teacup."

The chubby old nest-maid snake offered Doc Finebeak the teacup on her back. *I could get used to this*, he thought. Then corrected himself. *What do I mean "could"? I have gotten used to it. So refined.* His tracking nights were over, and he had to admit he loved retirement. How wonderful it was to perch in this hollow with this lovely owl and just sip tea. It had been love at first sight, for him at least, when they had met. *How long has it been now?* he thought. *Six, seven moon cycles ago?* It was during the time of the Golden Tree. Madame Plonk had been placed under house arrest for some stupid violation of the ember laws, or whatever they were called, but she had escaped to warn the Band about Otulissa, who was being held under arrest in the prison. It was a brave thing for the singer of the tree to do. She had not flown abroad for years. She was not used to stormy weather or the hardships of life on the wing in the wild. Her tracking and navigation skills were weak. She had been a singer, for Glaux's sake, and singing was her only duty at the great tree, singing and the musical instruction of the nest-maids of the grass harp guild. When Doc Finebeak had found her, she was one exhausted heap of feathers. But a beautiful one at that! When she had told him the vile things that were transpiring at the great tree he was determined to help her find the Band and the young king. What a bad time that had been, when the tree had remained unseasonably golden.

As if reading Doc Finebeak's mind, Madame Plonk said, "You know I've never thought I would enjoy tea in this cup again after . . . after . . ." She hesitated. "After all the trouble during the time of the Golden Tree. But honestly, I have never enjoyed tea in this cup so much."

"Why's that, my dear?"

"It's simple, Docky. Sharing it with you makes all the difference."

Just at that moment something hurled into the hollow.

"Help! I need your help, Doc, right now!"

Doc Finebeak, Madame Plonk, and blind Octavia

gaped at the mass of heaving feathers that was Pelli, the mate of Soren. "My chick," Pelli sobbed. "She's gone!"

Perhaps Octavia was the most stunned of all as, through wrenching sobs, Pelli told the story of what had happened to dear Bell, the spirited little daughter of Soren. *I should have felt it coming*, Octavia thought to herself. *What's happening to me? I should have known that an agitated mother owl was flying directly into this hollow — headwinds or not. My sense for vibrations isn't worth two pellets these days.*

"Now, calm yourself, my dear," Doc Finebeak was saying as Madame Plonk ran her beak through Pelli's flight feathers. They were littered with debris from flying through dirty weather at reckless speeds. "Are the other B's all right?"

"Oh, yes, thank Glaux. They are fine. They flew home beautifully. But little Bell. She's so tiny." Pelli gulped and tried to swallow her sobs. "You will go look for her, won't you, Doc?"

"How could you ever doubt that I would do anything but go? I shall leave immediately. This headwind that you encountered will be a tailwind for me and get me there in no time."

He turned to Octavia. "Octavia, my feather, please." He paused. "Ah, you already have it!"

Yes, she thought. At least she had anticipated this, been

right in her instincts that Doc Finebeak would, as he said, leave immediately. The black feather was that of a crow. Doc Finebeak was both loved and feared by crows, and many years before had brokered a bargain with these bullies of the sky who delighted in mobbing owls during lightday. The black crow feather that topped his white plumage gave him a pass to fly anywhere, any hour of the day or night, free from the threat of crows.

So handsome, Madame Plonk thought as she watched him fly off into the darkening night.

CHAPTER NINE

The River of Wind

Oh, you'll know it, Soren, don't worry. You'll know it when you get there. He certainly did know it. Mrs. Plithiver's words ran through his head now. One moment the world had been suffused with the light of day, and the next it was the pitch of night. The blackness had slammed down upon them like one of Bubo's hammers on the anvil. The stars were like sparks from hot iron being struck. They had arrived at the tomorrow line. No gaudy sunset dissolving slowly into First Lavender. No creeping gray before First Black. They were just there — into tomorrow.

"Uh . . ." Martin said. "We're at the tomorrow line, right, Mrs. P.?"

"Yes, dear. Quite dramatic, isn't it?"

"I would say that's an understatement," Otulissa replied. Did Soren detect in her voice a whiff of disdain?

Mrs. P. leaned over and whispered in Soren's ear slit. "You know Otulissa. She prefers logic to intuition. She is very distrustful of these leaps over reasoning. She has such an orderly mind."

"Yes," Soren agreed. "So what do we do now?"

Mrs. Plithiver made her coil tighter and rose slightly higher on Soren's back so she could address the owls. "Well, my dears . . ."

"I wish she wouldn't call us that," Otulissa muttered to Twilight. "I find it demeaning."

"Oh, put a mouse in it, Otulissa," Twilight huffed. "She's always called us 'dear' and 'dearie.' It's her way."

Mrs. Plithiver continued. "I think that key of yours might work now, Otulissa. I think it just might," Mrs. Plithiver said encouragingly.

"Terrific. Let me read the temperascope gauge and then . . ." She had not even finished the sentence when a slashing wind out of nowhere nearly whipped the device from her talons. This was followed by an onslaught of buffeting winds from all directions.

"Great Glaux!" Soren cried out. "We're in the windkins. Climb!"

These were winds like none they had ever experienced, not even the Shredders, those winds that savaged the border between the canyonlands and the Shadow Forest, which few owls except for the Guardians dared to fly.

"The temperature is falling!" Otulissa shouted out. "We must fly up. The symbol on the key says 'up' when air cools."

"Key! Key!" screeched Ruby. "Racdrops! Only flying is going to get us out of this." But Ruby herself, the greatest flier in the five known kingdoms, was struggling hard.

"There's a thermal upswing. I'm feeling it," Otulissa cried out. "Banking turn to starboard."

Crosscurrents, downdrafts, updrafts, wind pits, and thermal upswings whirled together violently to form a deadly vortex of winds.

"Stick close to us, Gylfie and Martin!" Soren called out. Together, Twilight and Soren had made a kind of storm kronkenbot, which they had used in the past to help protect tiny owls like Gylfie and Martin in violent weather. Mrs. P. herself tightened up her coil, but it was all she could do to keep from flopping around. Never had she experienced anything like this! *Oh, maybe snakes really do belong on the ground,* she thought. *Why do we blind snakes always long for the yonder, the sky? Would that I were a simpler reptile!*

"Oh, Great Glaux!" Ruby gave a terrifying shriek. "It's the tumblebones!" Flying out ahead of the others, she had just spotted a bird skull. With a bit of flesh and feather still attached, it appeared half mummified.

"Down! Down! Down!" Otulissa shouted. "Down, or we're dead!" The eight owls plunged at terrifying speeds, faster, even, than a kill spiral.

Do I have a gizzard? Mrs. Plithiver thought. *I swear it feels as if a gizzard's bouncing up to my head.*

"Catch her!" Soren screamed.

"Oh, Great Glaux in glaumora! I'm flying and I have no wings!" Mrs. P.'s hiss seared the air as she felt her once-tight coil unfurl. The soft feathers of Soren's ruff were gone. She was tumbling through the lacerating winds. "Oh, Glaux," she called out. "Another tumblebones!" A great blue heron, belly up, wings down, its face a death mask of unending agony, sailed by. Then she felt something clamp down on her.

"Great catch, Digger!" Twilight shouted.

"Brilliant," Ruby called out.

But Digger nearly went yeep. He began to plunge farther as he spied a piece of Mrs. P. go spinning off in the wind.

Mrs. Plithiver instantly knew what had happened as she hung from Digger's mouth. "Don't worry, Digger. Just a piece of my tail. Don't need it. I'm not a rattler."

"We're almost through the windkin," Otulissa gasped. "Just one more thermal layer to go through."

"Count off!" Coryn ordered. It had been decided before they left that immediately following a dangerous situation, they would count off to make sure all members of the expedition were accounted for by calling out their own names in alphabetical order.

"Coryn — here!"

"Digger — here!"

"Gylfie — here!"

"Martin — here!"

"Otulissa — here!"

"Mrs. P. — mostly here!"

"Ruby — here!"

"Soren — here!"

"Twilight — here!"

"Alter course!" Otulissa shouted. "Wings about! Hard alee!" This was the command for making a 180-degree turn. "Now, up and over the last ridge of the windkins!" Otulissa shouted triumphantly as she confirmed the last temperature change with the key now emblazoned forever in her brain. The owls, their plummels stripped from their wings' edges, staggered over this last rung of the violent windkin ladder and now tumbled gently into a soft, swift current of air untroubled by crosswinds.

It was perhaps ironic that it was Mrs. Plithiver, a

non-flying reptile, who named this tantalizing current the River of Wind. But the name stuck. Each one of the eight owls would describe differently that fabulous moment when they first encountered the River of Wind. In the beginning, it was just rills, tiny streamlets that ran off the river that brushed their wing tips and ruffled their remaining plummels like mere whispers. But then the owls were pulled into the flow, into the very center of the main current. At times it was boisterous, but more often than not, calm and gentle, and always swift.

The feeling of traveling in this current reminded Gylfie of a pale gray satin ribbon that Trader Mags had once brought for bartering. She had wanted it, but Madame Plonk had outbid her. The Snowy would fly with it on special occasions, and it would unfurl behind her, smooth and languid in the wind. But its texture was what had intrigued Gylfie. It was like touching the softest cool breeze. And for her that was exactly the feeling of the River of Wind.

For Soren, it brought memories of the down that Pelli plucked from her underfeathers for the three B's. For Martin, it was reminiscent of the high summer hollow his family had, which was nearly above the tree line on the mountains. There was a special moss that grew there that was even softer than rabbit's ear moss, and his mum would make their beds with it. For Twilight, it was like the echo of a song — a song from long ago. He could almost remember some of the words, but had no clue as to where they had come from. There had been a wonderful voice singing it, singing this song just for him. A voice like silk? Satin? Like liquid moonlight, it flowed, it curled around him and suffused him with a glowing warmth.

Overhead the stars drifted, and new constellations they had never seen before melted out of the night. Otulissa had been right. They barely needed to waggle a wing. This strong, warm, flowing wind pushed them along. They moved fast and effortlessly, traveling a great distance in what seemed like no time at all. They even took short naps. They were safe as long as they stayed in the central trough and avoided the edges. They did remain alert, however, to those edges as every once in a while a grim reminder of the danger that lurked within the wind-kins popped up — the mangled body of a seagull, the detached head of an eagle, and other assorted corpses that through some unknown process became slightly mummified, making them look all the more terrifying.

"It's like the living dead," Martin muttered as he caught sight of a tiny sparrow, its eyes frozen in horror in its still-feathered face. They were all rather relieved that so far they had not seen the remnant of Mrs. P.'s tail.

"What's that?" Ruby said.

"What?" Soren asked.

"Straight up," Ruby replied.

Mrs. Plithiver braced herself between Soren's shoulders because she knew what was coming — a maneuver only an owl could make because of the seven extra bones in its neck, which allowed it to swivel its head in a wide arc and flip it straight up; they all made the same movement at the same time. Now their faces were where the tops of their heads had been, seconds before. Mrs. P. looked up, too. *How very odd,* she thought.

"What is it?" Soren asked.

"Not a bird," Otulissa and Twilight both said at once.

"No, definitely not a bird," Digger replied.

"It's not a living thing," Mrs. Plithiver said. For had it been, she knew she would have detected the vibrations from the beats of its heart.

"But it's beautiful," Gylfie said as they all looked up at this colorful thing that danced and skipped above them in the eddies of the River of Wind.

It was triangular in shape and made of some sort of material — possibly parchment — that had been stretched over a frame. From the lower point of the triangle flew a tail, or perhaps it was a banner, made from brightly colored rags.

"Look! There's another!" Twilight said, spotting a second such contraption below them.

"There are strings attached! They lead downward." Coryn cried out. "Let's follow the strings!"

"Follow the strings!" they all cried out.

CHAPTER TEN

Conversations with a Blue Owl

B ut your feathers — why are they blue?" Bell asked as she finished a winter-skinny mouse. Normally, she would have scoffed at such fare. But this was the first food she had eaten since she had been spun out of the scuppers of the gale. Until now she had been too weak to eat anything of substance at all.

"And why are *your* feathers brown and the ones on your face white?" the blue owl replied. Striga's Hoolian had become more fluent as Bell, despite her condition, asked endless questions.

"Because my mum's and da's are," she answered.

The blue owl churred softly.

"Oh, I get it!" Bell said, her dark eyes sparkling. "Your mum and da were blue. So that's why you're blue." She seemed momentarily satisfied with this answer. But then the tiny delicate feathers on her brow began to pucker up.

Oh, dear. Here comes another question, the blue owl thought.

"But I've never seen a blue owl before."

"I think there must be a lot you haven't seen," the blue owl replied.

Bell nodded thoughtfully. "I guess so." There was another pause. "Is there a lot you haven't seen?"

"Well, I am older, of course. So I have seen more." *But,* he thought, *I have never seen a black-eyed owl.* He resisted saying this, however. In this part of the world it would open up too many questions.

"Tell me, what have you seen?" Bell asked.

The blue owl sighed. He had seen so much but yet so little. There was no way he could explain. He believed she was what they called in this world a Barn Owl. He had found that with this inquisitive little owl it was best to answer her questions with as few words as possible. It was better to just let her fill in with her own notions and ideas. It had actually worked quite well. First, the little owl whose name was Bell had quite by accident given him a name. When she had asked what he was he had merely answered with the generic name "Striga," which he knew his kind was called. She had assumed it was his personal name, and the blue owl loved it immediately that Bell had thus named him. He much preferred the name Striga to his real name, Orlando, which had always irked him. It

83

was one of those fussy, overly fancy, typical court names. Through such conversations, the blue owl was never really forced to lie outright.

Bell began to make assumptions derived from the short answers he gave her. He had artfully led her into believing that he was from a very remote part of the Northern Kingdoms and was a Glauxian Brother. Talking passed the time, and she was a pleasant little owl. Her port wing was badly damaged, and he knew it would be quite a while before Bell could fly home. And she did miss her home. She often woke up in the middle of the day crying for her mum or da or her two sisters. The blue owl had become quite fond of the little one. He would be sad to see her leave. He assumed that some owl would come looking for her. He liked to hear her talk of the great tree, but often it caused her to cry. He believed it was the very same tree he had heard of in whispers back home about what were called the Theo Papers.

He now heard a fluttering outside the tree hollow as the little owlet ate the skinny mouse he had brought her. He went to the rim of the hollow and peered out. He had had a feeling for a night or more that there was something out there, someone watching this hollow. But all was still. *It must be my imagination. Besides, I'm tired. So very tired.* He had arrived only a few nights before from the terminus of the Zong Phong. It was amazing that he had found his way out of it at this end, for there were no qui guides, but the windkins did not seem as fierce here. He simply had been dumped out of it unceremoniously, onto the shores of the Guanjho-Noh. He then had to fly what seemed like a much longer flight than the one he had just completed to get to this forest. And face it, owls of his background were not much good at flying. Riding the Zong Phong was one thing, but flying without a current to carry one along was quite another. He had only just arrived in the midst of a gale when Bell had fallen from the sky. His recollections were interrupted again by a sound close by. He was right. Someone was watching them.

"I don't believe it!" An owl with a huge face that gave the appearance of a ragged moon whispered to another Barn Owl with a large nick out of his beak. "A blue owl, I've never seen the likes."

"Nor I, General Mam."

"Nor I," three other owls replied in turn. Two of these owls were Barn Owls, the other was a Burrowing Owl.

"What's he got in there?"

"I think it's a wounded young owl who got tossed about in that gale," said the Burrowing Owl.

"You don't think it's one from those chawlet practices

you were monitoring, do you?" The owl with the huge face turned to the other three accompanying her.

The larger of the two Barn Owls replied, "Well, it's a far piece from Silverveil to here in Ambala. But that gale was part of the westers, and its winds could have blown the young one this far. You never can tell."

The moonfaced owl's eyes gleamed darkly. "Stryker, are you thinking what I'm thinking?" Stryker was the only one of the three other owls who would know what she was suggesting. Of the three owls accompanying the moonfaced Barn Owl, only he had been in battle — not once but three times — against the Guardians of Ga'Hoole.

"Well, yes, ma' — I mean, General Mam. It's almost too good to hope for."

"This isn't about hope, Stryker. This is about practical imagination. It's about making things happen. Any fool can hope. But it takes brains to imagine. And if you can't imagine, nothing will ever happen. I can make things happen. But I must admit, if it is indeed a Guardian owlet," she let her voice dwindle to a lower whisper, "well, what sweet justice would be served."

Nyra had not always felt the way she did about the role of imagination in her life. She had, in fact, thought it ridiculous and had often reprimanded her son, Nyroc (now called Coryn), for wandering off into all sorts of imaginative channels. But that was before she had discovered *The Book of Kreeth* — the ancient hagsfiend from the primeval world of owls. In this book she had learned of things that were unimaginable to ordinary owls. But Kreeth had been no ordinary owl: She had been a hagsfiend.

"Huh? I mean, huh, General Mam?" Nyra had lost Stryker on the sweet justice part.

She shook her head and with great sneering disdain said, "Don't you get it? They took my son. My chick. Now I will take theirs. And I do think it is theirs. I feel it in my gizzard. My gizzard's been feeling a lot better lately. It must be that herb mixture that you've been getting for me."

Stryker wilfed a bit. He didn't want to tell her that the last time he had gone to the herbalist in Kuneer, an Elf Owl, he had had to rough the fellow up a bit to get the medicine.

The moonfaced owl, Nyra, was the supreme commander of the Pure Ones. Stryker was her top lieutenant, although she had recently been thinking about replacing him. After too long a time, things were again looking up for the Pure Ones. The alliance with the wolves had proved to be a mistake, but one learns from mistakes.

Stick to owls — down-and-out owls. A series of forest fires had also proved a boon for Nyra. Owl families had been split apart; orphans were available for the snatching. And what could be snatched at an early enough age could be trained, indoctrinated, gizzard-washed until they were pliant, docile, and perfect for her growing army of Pure Ones. Those who were not orphans but adults, hollow-less adults who had been burned out of their homes and had lost their mates and families, could also be lured into the cadres of the Pure Ones, which offered support, the promise of leadership roles, and new responsibilities other than just the daily grind of providing fresh meat for one's family. Many found this, if not a welcome change, at least a way to forget that once upon a time they'd even had families. Most were so grief-stricken that any memory of their former life was searingly painful.

So Nyra had offered an alternative: the Desert of Kuneer. No trees, no forest fires. When displaced owls asked where they would live, Nyra explained the joys of burrows, although cactus dwelling was available. It was the Burrowing Owl Tarn, a sergeant, whom she was thinking of to replace Stryker. Tarn had been the architect of the extensive burrow system in Kuneer. It was now inhabited by the largest force of Pure Ones Nyra had managed to muster in a long time. It would be tricky, though, promoting Tarn, a non–Barn Owl, to such a high position. Technically, he was not a Pure One, but it was Tarn who had dug out their first encampment in a remote region in the Desert of Kuneer, supervised its continued expansion, and introduced them to the herbalist and healer Cuffyn, an Elf Owl. The odd but useful little owl lived in an immense cactus with several good-sized hollows, where he practiced medicinal arts.

So successful had Nyra's recruitment campaign been that she had even set a few fires herself in service to her cause — the rebuilding of the Pure Ones' empire. She liked to think of it as an "empire" although it had never been associated with any particular part of the owl kingdoms or geography for any length of time. *But things are going to be different now,* she thought as she watched the hollow where the peculiar blue owl tended some creature. *Yes, different!* And if her hunch was right, whatever was in that tree would be just what she needed to shift the winds completely in her favor. Nyra would wait and watch. According to Stryker, the blue owl was going out more often to hunt. Nyra would just wait and continue to watch patiently. Over time, she had learned patience, which had given her cunning an edge, tempered it to a fineness as deadly as the sharpest battle claws. And when the time was right, Nyra would strike.

CHAPTER ELEVEN

The Sage at the River's End

Following the strings, the owls descended through layers of clouds that had streaked through the River of Wind. Soon they spied high, jagged mountains, range upon range of icy peaks that appeared to march across this new continent that had appeared where the sea ended. Their eyes were fixed on the mountains directly ahead, and they neglected to see that just beneath them another landscape began to appear through a scrim of mist that was tossed up by the sea. Cliffs of pink-and-gray-swirled stone cascaded into the clouds of vapor. Occasionally, a notch in the cliffs revealed pine forests and boughs of trees laden with snow.

"Look! Look!" Twilight said excitedly. "Look down there!" The eight owls looked in the direction that Twilight was indicating with his starboard wing tip. Perched on a high rock outcropping was a large bird. The strings they were following down all seemed to stream from this one bird. Occasionally he would lift up into the air as if tugged by the contraptions at the sky end of the strings. As they descended, the owls could see that some of the strings were anchored to various rocks and the gnarled trunks of trees, many of which grew at odd angles from the rock outcropping. The bird was swooping back and forth, manipulating the various strings, when suddenly he grabbed what appeared to be a large hammer in his talons and flew up to a bronze disc that dangled from a vine. He hammered the disc and a resounding *gong* rang out, reverberating across the landscape to the distant mountains and causing clumps of snow to fall from the pine boughs.

"Welcome! Welcome! Hee naow, hee naow!"

"Oh, Glaux! He's speaking Jouzhen . . ." Otulissa muttered. "Hee naow, zan li," she answered.

"What's she saying?" Gylfie hissed.

"This is so exciting!" Soren swiveled his head around, trying to take in everything all at once. There was so much to see. "Have you ever seen trees like these? I mean, they look like pine trees, but their trunks are as gnarled as an old owl's talons."

"But beautiful," Gylfie said.

"Everything is so different," Coryn said, his voice soft with wonder.

"Yes," Digger replied. "Including that owl. He's blue!"

Perhaps it was because everything did seem so different that at first they did not notice the strange hue of the owl flying before them, who was shouting with apparent great glee, "Hee naow! Welcome!" every few seconds.

"I mean, he is an owl, isn't he?" Gylfie asked as she and the others alighted onto the rock ledge.

"Oh, yes, I am an owl. Welcome. I have been expecting you."

They all blinked. "You have?" Otulissa said. The owl nodded. Otulissa then stepped forward and began to introduce herself and the rest with her rudimentary Middle Kingdom language skills. "Shing zao strezhing Ga'Hoole."

"Oh, no need to speak Jouzhen. I have been studying Hoolian for many years in anticipation of this evening." He spoke with a delightful musical cadence. Mrs. Plithiver found herself swaying to its rhythm as if she were entwined in the strings of the grass harp, awaiting her cue to jump an octave or two.

"So you are the owls of Ga'Hoole, and I am Tengshu, the qui dong of the cliffs of the luminous pearl gates to our kingdom. Here the Zong Phong ends and the Jouzhenkyn begins."

"Qui dong?" Otulissa asked. "What is a 'qui dong'?" The words sounded so basic, yet so important. She wondered why she and Bess had not found them for the dictionary they had composed.

"Your interest in our language impresses me, pheng gwuil."

Otulissa knew that "pheng" was the word for "honored," and "gwuil" was the word for "guest." "The word 'dong,'" the owl continued, "is the word for 'knower' or 'sage.' But 'qui' is harder to explain in Hoolian, for I do not think you have such a contrivance," he said, nodding toward the triangle and the string, which he was now winding in on a spool. As the colorful qui came closer, they saw that it was made of very thin parchment that had been decorated with beautiful designs.

"Contrivance?" Coryn asked.

"Yes, Your Majesty."

Now they were all stunned. How did Tengshu know that Coryn was their king? Coryn made a point of never wearing any royal trappings, and he had even discarded the ceremonial cloaks that the old King Boron and Queen Baran had sometimes worn.

"But this contrivance," Coryn persisted, "it might have an associated name that we may know."

"But how could it have a name if it does not exist for you?" Tengshu asked.

Digger cocked his head. This was a most interesting

philosophical question. There could be no name if there was no object to be named, and the eight owls plus one nest-maid snake had never in all their days seen anything like this contrivance, this "qui," as Tengshu called it.

"This one is called the qui of the dancing frog."

What in the world were these qui contrivances for? Why was Tengshu blue? And how had he known they were coming? Questions swirled in the minds of the owls like the flurries of snow that had begun to blow.

"Come ... come to my hollow." Tengshu motioned to them and took the qui of the dancing frog in his talon with its string and tail neatly bound up. They followed him, flying through a narrow fissure between two sheer cliffs of stone. Beneath them as they flew, a valley opened out and the floor of this valley rose as they flew on, until it ended just beneath a series of ledges on which a small grove of trees grew.

"Trees growing out of rock," Soren said. "I've never seen such a thing."

"Oh, our trees are tough here. They can grow from anything," Tengshu said.

It was in one of these tall, twisted, old trees that Tengshu the knower, the sage, lived. The owls of Ga'Hoole, however, were in for yet another surprise.

They could clearly see that the tree had hollows, but from its branches several platforms were suspended with vines.

Tengshu alighted on one of the platforms. The eight owls followed, stepping tentatively toward a small table already set with cups made from an odd material that they did not recognize. Mrs. Plithiver slithered off Soren's back. She began to coil herself up and then slipped a bit awkwardly to one side. She was not accustomed to dealing with the shortened length of her body.

"Oh, pardon me," she said softly. "Lost a bit of my tail. You know. Rough flight."

Tengshu cocked his head. "I am sorry, but perhaps I can help you with that. I have some herbs that are quite good for healing breaks and ruptures of all sorts. The windkins can be hard, I know."

"You can say that again," Martin muttered under his breath.

"But the ones at this end of the stream are not so bad, are they?"

"Not bad at all," Otulissa replied.

"You see, when you fly out of the main current, the Zong Phong, as we call it, it's just an easy descent at this end. And my qui strings make for a good path. Now, excuse me for one moment, please."

A few minutes later, Tengshu returned with a steaming bowl. "Mountain tea. And I beg your indulgence for just one more moment," he said, setting down the bowl. He then returned with a second bowl and placed it next to Mrs. Plithiver. "Just put the end of your tail in that, madam, and I think you will find it quite soothing." He then turned and said, "Welcome to my hollow."

The owls nodded politely, but this wasn't exactly a hollow.

Coryn stepped forward. He blinked. "First, we would like to present you with a gift from our side of the world, that of the Five Kingdoms. In one region, a special kind of moss is plentiful and is highly valued. We call it rabbit's ear moss because it is as soft as the fur that grows inside the ears of rabbits. We hope you will enjoy it." Coryn placed a botkin of the moss on the table.

"That is most kind of you, honorable owl of the Five Kingdoms." The sage bowed deeply. "A bit of softness is always a welcome thing."

Coryn continued, "We have seen many new things in the short time we have been here. Everything seems so new and different to us, and we have many questions. Can you tell us why you call this your hollow? We are not inside a tree but ... but ..." Coryn looked around. "This, I believe, is another object for which we might not have the correct name. We would call this a platform. We have one for taking tea in the branches of the great tree."

"It is a platform, you are right, and as you see, we are taking tea. But it is really my moon-viewing platform, and on the other side of the tree, from which I can see the Guanjho-Noh, is my wave-viewing platform."

"Guanjho-Noh?" Otulissa asked. "'Noh' means 'sea,' doesn't it?"

"Yes, indeed it does. It is the sea that lies between the Middle Kingdom and where you come from — the Fifth World of owls. 'Guanjho' means 'vastness.' We call it the Sea of Vastness. You are good with languages, I see," he said, nodding at Otulissa.

"Yes. I am considered somewhat of a linguist."

The seven other owls exchanged surreptitious glances. *Don't get her going,* Soren thought.

"Now perch and have some tea."

"If a simple nest-maid snake might ask a question, sir." Mrs. Plithiver had suspended herself from one of the platform's vines.

"Of course."

"Well, being in the domestic arts, I notice that you serve your own tea. It's really quite a nice spread you've laid out for us." Indeed, there were tiny savory buns, and frogs that appeared to have been wrapped in little nets of woven pine needles and then smoked. "I say, you do this all by yourself? No nest-maids?"

"I am self-sufficient, madam. I choose not to have any servants. I am what you might call, in your language, a hermit." This term the owls did know. "I find that I can think better if I live a solitary life and one of simplicity."

Gylfie looked down at the tightly bound smoked frogs in their beautifully woven pine-needle jackets. *You call this simple?* she thought.

"And you are," Digger continued, "a knower of these qui contraptions?"

"Yes, and you must wonder what they are used for." Once again the owls nodded. "They have a purpose and they have not," Tengshu said cryptically. "You see, it is often for sheer joy that one flies a qui, and joy is not considered a practical thing in most societies — although I disagree. However, when I fly my qui I am most often seeking information."

"Information?" Soren asked. "What kind of information?"

"Oh, there is so much to be learned from flying qui. After all, I cannot be everywhere at once. With the qui I can detect all manner of wind currents, speed, moisture in clouds" — he hesitated as if searching for the right word — "and jing jangs — I think you might call them hail cusps."

"Hail cusps!" Otulissa and Soren both burst out at once. These were furrows in the air where hailstones formed. "You mean," Soren said excitedly, "you get weather information from these qui?"

"Yes, and more."

"More?" Gylfie said.

"Of course. For what we take, we must give back."

The eight owls blinked.

"What do you give back?" Coryn asked.

"Our thanks to Glaux. We send our prayers up. I write a poem or send one of my paintings."

"You paint?"

"Oh, yes. Come inside now and I shall show you some of my paintings."

The owls followed Tengshu.

"What is this?" Gylfie gasped as she flipped her head so she was looking straight up. From the ceiling of the hollow hung scrolls painted with beautiful scenes of mountains and waterfalls, birds and flowers. There was one of crashing waves and another of a still pond with a heron standing at its edge.

"Is this parchment paper?" Soren asked.

"No. I paint on silk. There is a mulberry tree with a silk league not far from here."

"A silk league?" Mrs. Plithiver asked, suddenly alert. There was, of course, no way she could see the pictures, but the notion of using silk was very interesting to her.

"Yes, indeed. Blind snakes, like yourself, collect the cocoons made by the silkworms of the tree. They then unravel them into long threads and weave them together. Of course, before the cloth is ready to be painted they must beat it until its finish is smooth. It is a long and complicated process. But the silk league from whom I get my pieces is one of the finest."

"Rather like the weavers guild back at our tree," Mrs. Plithiver offered.

"Yes, I have heard of that guild," Tengshu replied.

The owls were stunned. This was yet another indication that Tengshu knew more about them than they knew about him.

"How do you know all this?" Otulissa blurted out. "You knew we were coming. You know far more of our Hoolian language than any of us knows of yours, and now you tell us that you know about the weavers guild."

The sage blinked calmly. In the dim light of the hollow, his plumage did not seem quite so blue. He took a few short hops to a bowl made from the same material as the cups from which they had just drunk. A wick floated in the bowl, and from a small flask he drew out a piece of raw ore and struck it against a flintstone. A small flame started in a pile of kindling. He then took a burning twig and lit the wick. A slightly acrid smell began to suffuse the air. "Yak butter — I don't think you are familiar with that animal — but it is of vital importance to the owls of the Middle Kingdom." He paused. "Now, I know you are brimming with questions. So find yourselves a perch and I will try to explain as much as I can."

The eight birds set down on various perches. Mrs. Plithiver settled herself into a relaxed coil near the yak-butter lamp, which cast a soft glow.

"I shall address your last two points first. How do we know about the great tree's weavers guild, and how do I know Hoolian? It was all written in the Theo Papers."

"Theo!" Otulissa exclaimed, and lofted slightly into the air. It was as if a bolt of lightning had shot through her.

"Theo, the first blacksmith?" Coryn gasped.

"Theo, the inventor of battle claws?" Twilight said excitedly.

"Theo, the gizzard-resister?" Digger asked.

The sage nodded.

Otulissa could hardly recover her wits to sort out all of her questions. *But of course*, she thought. *It's beginning to make perfect sense that Theo came here!* Otulissa had done further research inspired by reading the legends. It had seemed to her with a little reading between the lines that Theo had flown far away to some unknown place, but she had discounted this as idle speculation. Nonetheless, he seemed to have vanished. Now, however, there was much evidence pointing to where he might have gone. They had quickly recognized the weather symbols of the key to be a more ancient form of their own weather symbols. And who had been the first real weather interpreter? None other than Joss, a contemporary of Theo's and renowned scout and messenger for the H'rathian Kingdom in the time of the legends. There were other similarities as well. Certain Jouzhen words seemed to come from Krakish root words, but with a slight twist. The word "strezhing," which she had used in her introductory greeting, meant "originating from or hailing from." In Krakish, one said "Stresschen," which basically meant the same thing. "So did Theo really come here?" Otulissa said with awe.

"Oh, yes." The sage nodded. "And he wrote a very long document that we call the Theo Papers. It was from reading the papers that I first learned of the Great Ga'Hoole Tree and the brilliant King Hoole."

Otulissa and Soren exchanged quick glances. "Did you read the legends?" Soren asked.

"Legends?" Tengshu seemed slightly confused. "Oh, no. These were real stories."

"Legends can be real," Coryn added in a low voice. "Did he write of the ember?"

"Oh, perhaps a bit," the sage said almost dismissively. "He mostly wrote of the ways of war and his determination never to make another weapon. He sought another way. He called it 'the way without claws.' It has come to be known as 'the way of noble gentleness' or 'Danyar.' By and large, the Theo Papers are really philosophical documents."

"Did he ever return to the Five Kingdoms?" Digger asked.

"Not that anyone knew of," Tengshu replied. "He remained at the owlery. There was much to do there."

"The owlery?"

"It is a place high, high up in the tallest mountains of Jouzhenkyn where owls who desire a simpler way of living and deep contemplation retreat. Unlike myself, they do not enjoy pursuing this life in solitude. But before Theo came, it was a place of no real discipline, and one of shallow thought at best. But at least it was different from court life. When Theo came he changed this. He began to teach the way of noble gentleness."

"But how did you know we were coming here?" Coryn asked.

"It was predicted by the eighth astrologer, the astrologer of the old court."

"The old court? Astrology?" Otulissa was perplexed. She considered astrology to be a slightly yoicks discipline that should not even be considered a science. It was seldom practiced in the Hoolian world. "What is this court? Do you have a king, a royal family?"

"Not really. Or, I should say, not real ones, not any longer."

The owls looked confused.

Tengshu continued. "Once we did have a court but it became useless and, in its uselessness, even dangerous. The owls who started the owlery did so to escape the court. So now we have a mock court. Well, it is a bit more than that."

"A mock court? What are you talking about?" Gylfie asked. This new world, this Middle Kingdom, was proving more bewildering than any of them could have ever imagined.

"You'll see . . . you'll see," Tengshu churred softly. "I

know it is all very confusing. But you have entered a new world. It is very different from yours, so I am told."

Told. The word rang in Mrs. Plithiver's head. She had begun experiencing odd sensations about this owl as soon as they had entered the hollow. She sensed that there was a kind of sad mist hovering in this owl's gizzard, a sense of loss, perhaps of grief.

"Tell me, sir . . . ," Mrs. Plithiver asked, "and I hope it is not too intrusive of me to ask such a question. . . ."

"If it is, I shall not answer, " the sage replied simply.

"Does all of your knowledge of our world come from your study of the Theo Papers, or did you ever visit it?"

"Oh, no. I never visited it." His voice began to quake a bit. He paused. "But someone very close to me did — my mother."

"Your mother?" Coryn asked.

"Yes, but that was long, long ago. Let's see, I think it was not that long after the time of King Hoole."

"King Hoole!" they all exclaimed.

"B-b-b-but . . . sir," Gylfie stammered, "that is impossible. That would have been hundreds of years ago. Surely your mother was not alive back then?"

"Oh, but you don't understand. We live a very long time here. I am — let's see — about three hundred and twenty-five years old. At the owlery, they live close to four hundred years. I believe there is a pikyu who is four hundred and twenty. The dragon owls of the mock court in the Panqua Palace don't usually live as long. It depends."

"Dragon owls?" They gasped.

"Pikyu?" Coryn asked.

"Yes, pikyu is what we call our spiritual teachers. It really means 'guide.' Pikyus have, through long study and meditation, achieved deep wisdom. The word means just that — deep wisdom. You will see that within the pale yellow light of the pikyus' eyes, there are glints of green. Such is the sign of deep wisdom."

Four-hundred-year-old owls . . . ? Panqua Palace . . . dragon owls . . . ? Soren wondered. *Where in the world are we?*

CHAPTER TWELVE

The Hagbogey

Now, there you go, dear! Back with Mum and Da!"
Eglantine said as she dropped the little Barn Owl
into her family's hollow in the spruce tree in the forest of
Ambala. The owlet shreed with delight. The mother was
hysterical, and the father gruff but obviously relieved. For
several nights, Eglantine and Primrose had scoured every
wind track left by the westers that had marched across a
great swath of the kingdoms. The main track appeared to
run straight out of Silverveil, sweeping through The
Barrens and into Ambala. But so far they had found not a
trace of Bell. Nothing really, except this little Barn Owl
who had fallen to the ground because she had tried to fly
too soon, before even a single one of her flight feathers
had budged.

"Now, you ain't going to try that again are you, Eva?
No more flying until you're ready. You're a Barn Owl.
Not an Elf Owl, after all. Takes us sixty-six nights to fledge
our flight feathers," the father stated a bit sternly.

"Oh, we were so worried." The mother was still sobbing. She lowered her voice and blinked. "What with the rumors and all."

"Rumors? What kind of rumors?" Primrose asked.

"Nyra is back," she whispered, "and several snatchings and even egg-nappings have been reported."

Primrose and Eglantine exchanged nervous glances. No, it simply could not be true. There had been no sign of the Pure Ones in a long while. But this news made finding Bell even more urgent than before.

Eglantine and Primrose had been so excited when they had first spotted the distinctive yarped pellet of a young Barn Owl. They were sure it was Bell, and although they were happy to rescue this little owlet, Eva, they had to admit their disappointment that she was not Bell. Just another owl chick who had disobeyed the single most important rule for nestlings: Never fly before you are ready and never fly when your parents are out hunting. They bid the parents and the little chick good-bye.

"And where will you go from here?" the father asked.

"Well," Primrose said, "we're looking for a little owl who could fly, but perhaps not strongly enough. She got lost or blown down when those westers came through."

"Oh, those westers came through Ambala, all right.

Although they weakened some, I'm sure, as they approached the Desert of Kuneer."

"Yes, well," Eglantine said, "I think we have to go at least that far."

"Good luck to you both and thanks ever so much," the father said. Then the mother added, "Ever so much."

"Thank you," Eva said in a tiny voice. "I'm . . . I'm very sorry."

As Eglantine and Primrose flew on, their search became increasingly frustrating. Most of the fresh wind tracks had vanished by now. But they kept at it. While Eglantine flew the upper levels, Primrose flew quite low, perhaps only two feet above the ground, to look for talon prints or the telltale tufts of down that might have fetched up in low-growing scrub plants. Primrose was flying even closer when she caught sight of something odd in the bushes. *A feather? No,* she thought. *Couldn't be. Well, maybe a jay feather . . . but . . .*

"Eglantine!" She flipped her head straight up. "Come down here this instant! Wait'll you see this!"

Eglantine alighted near the bush where a blue feather was impaled on a thorny branch quivering in the ground breeze.

"It's owl!" Primrose said.

"It can't be! It's blue!"

"I know an owl feather when I see one and so do you." The tiny Pygmy Owl stomped her talons on the ground. "If this isn't an owl feather, I'll eat my trousers." Eglantine stepped closer and peered at the bright blue feather. "It certainly does look like an owl feather. But blue!"

"It's a median port wing covert," Primrose said. "But how do you explain this color?"

"A kraal?" Eglantine looked up and blinked.

"Kraals this far south? Besides, this isn't paint. This is real — a real, natural color." Kraals were the pirate owls of the Northern Kingdoms who painted their plumage gaudy colors. Primrose delicately extricated the feather from the thorn.

"It's a molted feather. I mean, it doesn't look as if it was torn off in a skirmish or anything," Eglantine said, as Primrose dropped the feather on the ground so they could better examine it.

"Yes, but it's really weathered — right down to its barbs," Primrose said. The barbs and barbules were the minuscule interlocking hooks that ran diagonally down a feather to make its surface smooth and functional. These had been worn away, leaving a fuzzy surface to the feather.

"This feather has had a long flight." Eglantine was bent

over, examining it closely. There was a queasy squirm deep in Eglantine's gizzard. She sighed. "Well, standing here on the ground isn't going to get us any closer to Bell. But maybe we should try and follow any signs of this blue owl and see if the track might lead to Bell . . . ," she paused, ". . . in some way." *Poor Bell*, she thought. *Where could that little owl be?* Eglantine herself had once been a lost owlet. A victim of the Great Downing. Twice owl-napped, first by the Pure Ones, and the second time by St. Aggie's. However, she managed to survive. She knew all too well the frightening feelings that a wounded, flightless owlet could experience when it was "ground bound," the countless hours looking up and wondering if she would ever be part of that sky world.

Eglantine and Primrose were still in the middle of Ambala and had to fight an increasing headwind as they flew east. They had promised themselves that they would fly at least as far as the desert. But the two owls were growing very tired. This was their fifth night of searching. What few wind tracks were left had begun to feel the same. With each wing stroke forward it seemed that the easterly wind pushed them back half a stroke. But how could they stop? This was Bell, precious Bell. Eglantine's niece. Soren's dear little daughter.

*   *   *

In the easternmost region of Ambala, Bell waited for the blue owl. Striga had been gone for the better part of the night on his hunting expedition. Bell had to admit that this blue owl was not the most proficient hunter. The bodies of mice and voles and squirrels that he brought back were badly mangled, as if he had very little experience. At one time, he had said something about how he had led a rather vain life. "One of luxury and impracticality" was how he described it. "Until you were a Glauxian Brother, that is?" Bell offered, and he merely nodded, replying, "I missed those early years when one learns the basics."

Striga cautioned Bell about what he called false Glauxes of luxury and refinement, and the pitfall of vanity. He even scolded her once when, bored with her days of confinement, she had strung some red berries onto one of his molted feathers. The berries were from a stash a squirrel had left behind in the hollow. Bell had thought the bright red against the blue of his feathers looked quite pretty, but Striga was completely scornful of what he called such "stupid and outrageous vanity." He threw the thing out of the hollow.

Nonetheless, he felt a great affection for the little Barn Owl. When she slept, he often watched her. For Striga, she represented the vigorous, wholesome life he had yearned for but never had. In the days and nights of caring for her, putting her needs before his own, and suffering the privations of life in the rustic hollow, a hope dawned in his gizzard: Maybe this little owl could be his redemption. Maybe he could do more than just wait for the completion of the cycle of his fate. They said there were no shortcuts. But there were — there had to be. He was a good owl now, no matter what he had been before. He could change his fate. This was his chance.

Other owls had mourned their existence at Panqua Palace, Striga reasoned further. But that was all they did: mourn. They had not become sickened, literally sickened, by the excess as he had: the jewels, the rubies, the sapphires, the constant preening of their glorious feathers, feathers as brilliant as the jewels that imprisoned them. While those owls had grown fat and ungainly, had he not lost weight? While their feathers grew long, had he not cut his? It was a sign that he was different. That his spirit was more refined. He knew that some force had chosen him, some force even greater than that of fate had dared him to change his destiny. So he had defied them. He had escaped, borne by the Zong Phong, into a new world. And now this little owlet, whom he had saved, confirmed to him that he was chosen for something else, something grander than the antiquated notions that governed the owls of Panqua, notions that they merely subscribed to and had no power to change. Well, he had power. And his mission must now be to warn others of the deadliness of excess, luxury, and the vanities. This was his duty, his sacred duty, and by fulfilling it, he would free himself.

But he was no fool. He still had much to learn. And why not, given the life he had led? It was embarrassing that this little owlet who called herself Bell knew so much more about hunting than he did. Earlier today when he had brought back an especially mangled mouse, she had asked if he had lost altitude too fast at the beginning of his kill spiral. The kill spiral is the plunging dive that an owl makes as it closes in on prey. Striga was completely ignorant of such a maneuver. "Kill spiral?" He had blinked. Bell explained in more detail.

"Yes, it's important to keep it very tight. You do it by using your wing tip as a pivot. You drill the air. That's the expression." Bell had nodded authoritatively.

"Sounds complicated."

"No, not really. Takes some practice. But I learned it really fast, faster than my two sisters, and I'm the smallest of the lot."

Bell, too, remembered the hunting tips she'd given Striga earlier. Her eyes had brimmed with tears when she mentioned her sisters. Now, as he was off hunting again, she felt herself getting all weepy just thinking about them. She sniffed and tried to think of something else to pass the time until Striga returned from the hunt. *Imagine,* she thought, *me teaching a grown-up owl about the kill spiral. Blythe and Bash won't believe it!* A sob welled in her gizzard. She swallowed. Would she ever see them again? And Mum and Da? Her wing felt a lot better. Maybe she could try just a short flight. A teeny-weeny one. She stepped tentatively out of the hollow. *I'll start with branching. Just the way I did when I was little in the days leading up to my first flight ceremony.*

She hopped to the nearest branch. Then hopped again and again.

Only two trees over from where Bell was testing her strength, in the thick, gnarled branches of an oak, an owl with weathered, ragged wings and a huge moon face watched the little owl's progress. "Will you look at that!" Nyra whispered to herself. *Amazing,* she thought. *Same speckled pattern around the fringes of her facial disk. Same tilt to her eyes. That's Soren's chick — I'll stake my gizzard on that.*

There was no time to think. One minute Bell was hopping from branch to branch. She paused to waggle her port wing a bit and was thinking that it was still a bit sore when a horrendous glaring disk appeared in front of her from out of nowhere. It looked as if the moon had fallen from the sky. The thought flashed through her mind, *It's the hagbogey!* Her gizzard cringed and twisted painfully. She yelped, then felt talons wrap around her.

CHAPTER THIRTEEN

The Ember, the King, and an Owlet!

The blue owl had been eager to show Bell the vole. He had successfully executed the kill spiral just as she had described it and was very proud of the prey he now gripped in his talons as he approached the hollow. She was a sweet little owl. They could both learn from each other — he about hunting and she about the dangers of being seduced by silly vanities. "Bell," he called out as he alighted on the branch just beneath their hollow. "Bell," he called again. *How odd*, he thought. He poked his head into the hollow. It was empty. "Bell!" And then before he could think, something swooped down upon him. Two white faces. *Barn Owls!* he thought. *They must be Bell's parents.*

The owls had appeared out of nowhere. There was one on either side of him, seizing each of his wings. Their talons didn't look like talons, more like long claws. They were shiny and caught the glint of the stars.

"I tried to help her. Don't hurt me. She's fine, isn't she? She wanted to get back to you as soon as she could," the blue owl wailed.

"Shut your beak. You're coming with us," said the larger of the two Barn Owls.

"But I don't understand. . . . You're her parents, aren't you?" Then Striga became so agitated that the Hoolian he had acquired since rescuing Bell seemed to vanish. He lapsed into Jouzhen.

"What in hagsmire is he babbling about, Stryker?" the other Barn Owl said.

A third owl appeared. Not white, and the legs were long, featherless, and very strong. He stormed into the hollow and bellowed at the Barn Owls holding Striga. "Everything under control here, Lieutenant Stryker and Corporal Wort?"

"Yes, Sergeant Tarn," the two Barn Owls barked in unison.

"Good. General Mam has flown on with the little one. She can handle the owlet on her own, but sent me back to help with this one. We're to take him back — in one piece. General Mam has some questions to ask this . . . this thing." He looked at the blue owl with contempt. The Burrowing Owl, Sergeant Tarn, and the two Barn Owls, Lieutenant Stryker and Corporal Wort, had been on this stakeout for the past three days, observing the blue owl and the little one who General Mam felt sure was the daughter of Soren. They had planned a two-phase strike. Phase one — Operation Owlet; phase two — Operation Blue Owl. First, they waited until the blue owl had gone hunting, at which time Nyra and the Burrowing Owl went in to snatch the owlet while Stryker and Wort flew lookout for the return of the blue owl. When the blue owl came back, Stryker and Wort hit. It was always better to attack while the target was in a confined space.

"Tether him, will you, Sergeant?" Stryker said. "Wort, you fly starboard. I'll fly port; Tarn, the rear. It should work. Wind's down. We'll take a straight-on route to the desert. Nice thermals coming off the sand. Should be an easy flight."

They had not been flying long, however, when the three owls realized that the blue owl was quickly tiring despite the warm thermal updrafts helping them.

"What's going on with this blue idiot? He can hardly fly," Corporal Wort muttered.

"I'm not used to it," the blue owl whined.

"Not used to it? Where you from?" Stryker demanded.

Striga clamped his beak tightly shut. Stryker did not feel like roughing him up right now. It would only make him slower. General Mam wanted him back in one piece, as she had said. She had very persuasive methods of making owls talk. He was sure she would get the information she needed.

The blue owl looked down. The forest was growing thinner. The tree line became fainter and receded behind them. The ground below turned hard and scrabbly, dotted with a few clumps of dusty low-growing shrubs. There were no cliffs, no canyons, no trees, and it was hard to imagine where an owl might live. Perhaps there were caves. He found himself thinking almost longingly of the place from which he had escaped, the Dragon Court of the Panqua Palace.

No! No! he scolded himself. He would never go back. He felt a quickening in his gizzard, and a strength began to flow through his hollow bones. But he must disguise it; they must continue to think of him as a weak, distracted, babbling owl. He would tell them nothing, but he would save that little Barn Owl. His life, which had not been a life at all but rather a living death, finally had meaning, purpose.

Eglantine dived toward the bush, carefully avoiding its sharp thorns, and plucked the feather from it. "This is Bell's feather. I'd recognize it anywhere. She has that russet brown in the fringe feathers of her face just like her mum. And look, the trail is absolutely clear — blue feathers mixed with a Barn Owl's. That blue owl must have snatched her."

"I'm not so sure about that," Primrose said. "Look at these broken feather shafts. I don't think Bell could have fought back to the point of breaking this owl's feathers. I think the Blue Owl might be a victim, too."

"Well, one thing is clear. They seem to be heading for the desert. I don't think we have any choice but to continue," Eglantine said, further examining the feathers.

"Should we send for reinforcements?" Primrose asked.

"I think we have to find out more first," Eglantine concluded.

Being experts in search-and-rescue and familiar with tracking techniques, both owls were not only experienced in uncovering tracks but in covering up their own. Stealth was part and parcel of any rescue or tracking operation. Whatever owls had abducted Bell and the blue owl had done their work in the sloppiest manner imaginable. In fact, as soon as they had come across the hollow where the owl-napping took place, it was simple to follow the track. Eglantine and Primrose were not sloppy owls. They would fly low but fast. If necessary they would use camouflage. Although few trees grew in this desert, there were plenty of scrubby bushes.

They flew a dark sky for the better part of the night, as the moon was still young in the newing. The track of the abductors had extended far into the southeastern section, avoiding the more heavily populated regions of the desert, where there were scores of Burrowing Owl settlements as well as cactus hollows for smaller owls.

"We need to get higher and look down. I can see the trail clearly. Great Glaux, these fellows are messy fliers. There's tumble feather all over the place," Eglantine said. The downy underfeathers were only shed if the owl was a noisy flier, which also meant the owl was a messy flier. She felt a slow dread creeping through her gizzard. The Pure Ones were just such fliers — strong, fast, and incredibly sloppy. Eglantine and Primrose clawed against a stiff headwind to a higher altitude but then found a buoyant warm thermal that gave them a good boost. Here they virtually soared, never having to flap a wing as they examined the landscape below.

"I'm seeing a pattern," Eglantine said as they flew over the easternmost region of the Desert of Kuneer. "Look at those humps in the sand. I'll wager there's a mess of burrows down there, more or less connected."

"If Digger were here, he'd know how to get in."

"Well, he's not," Eglantine said tersely. "We're going to have to figure this one out for ourselves."

"Look," Primrose said. "There's an owl flying low and it's heading for that rock."

Eglantine, however, had heard something even before Primrose had spied this low-flying owl. She was angling her head this way and that as they flew. Tilting her ear slits, she scanned what was quickly becoming a narrow vector from which vibrations were issuing. She listened as only a Barn Owl can. Barn Owls were known for their extraordinary hearing abilities, superior to those of most owls. She had already sifted through a hodgepodge of irrelevant noises, from the slitherings of a rattlesnake through the sand to the gasp of a rabbit as a desert bobcat sank its fangs into its back. She could even hear the snap of that rabbit's spine as it was torn apart, the trickle of its blood, the weakening pulse, and then the crunching of the bobcat's teeth. But through all this, she heard something much more alarming and familiar. Not words yet, but a vibration, a tone that she recognized.

"She's down there!" Eglantine whispered as she began a banking turn. Primrose followed in Eglantine's wind groove as she carved the turn.

"Who?"

"Nyra."

"Great Glaux!" Primrose's gizzard clenched. "But if we can hear her, she might be able to hear us."

"Doubtful. The Pure Ones listen as sloppily as they fly. Besides, we're in the better position. These rocks are streaked with long fissures. They are great for transmitting sound above the ground. I have an idea ... a plan." They alighted on a rock not far from the one toward which they had seen the low-flying owl heading.

The plan was not spoken aloud. To be very safe, Eglantine reverted to a series of signs — wing signing, it was called. By making various subtle tilts and shifts of their wings, the Guardians could communicate when they did not want their voices heard. It had been developed by the Band and Otulissa after they had become members of parliament. For years as youngsters, the Band and Otulissa had eavesdropped on the parliament by "going to the roots," as they called it. Once they became members of the parliament they feared that others might go to the roots and eavesdrop on them in turn, so the Band developed this silent way of communicating, which they taught to the other members as they joined the parliament. They only used it when they had to discuss the most sensitive issues and then adapted it to be used in other situations as well. Fortunately for Eglantine, these rocks possessed a powerful resonance, and with her acute hearing, the sound from beneath was transmitted with reasonable clarity.

"He can't hold out much longer ... he'll talk. Tarn, do you have that serum from the healer?"

Primrose and Eglantine stood just under a ledge of the rock on the opposite side from where they had seen the owl enter. The words came through with increasing clarity. Other sounds came through as well, agonizing ones of an owl gasping in pain, and then the soft mewlings of dear little Bell. Glaux knew what they were doing to her!

"I repeat, where are you from, blue owl? We want to know. Did you come from where we think the Chaw of Chaws went? My scouts followed them to the edge of the Beyond to the sea. Do you know Soren?" There was a loud wail as Bell heard her father's name. And Eglantine herself almost yelped. She and Primrose were no longer the only ones who knew where the Chaw of Chaws had gone. Nyra knew. Maybe this blue owl was from this new kingdom? What else could explain his peculiar plumage of blue and sapphire hues? Such feather colors were unknown in the Five Kingdoms.

Then two terrible words slithered up through the rock. "Slink melf." Eglantine and Primrose felt their gizzards turn to stone. Slink melf was the Pure Ones' expression for assassination squad. Eglantine signaled Primrose. In wing talk she indicated that now, while Nyra and her cohorts were in the burrows, they should make a brief reconnaissance of the nearby region. "To determine how far this encampment goes and pick up on other voices," Eglantine signaled. They would have to find out what kind of force Nyra had in readiness and somehow get word to Soren and the others.

They again flew low and close to the ground. Primrose, like so many tiny owls, was an expert low-altitude flier. Her skimming flight could take her mere inches above the ground. Eglantine flew a few feet higher. The combination was formidable. Between Primrose's skimming flight and Eglantine's superb hearing, they gathered a wealth of information not only pertaining to the extent of the Pure Ones' encampment but also to the intentions of their leader. Nyra had lusted for the Ember of Hoole since Coryn retrieved it from the Beyond. To have the Chaw of Chaws separated from the tree in a far and distant land was perfect. It was obvious that she had somehow raised a substantial army and hidden them here. Kuneer was riddled with bunkers. As Eglantine and Primrose listened carefully, they picked up the hum of throngs of owls chattering beneath these desert sands in this, the most isolated region of Kuneer. It had to be the Pure Ones.

If Nyra follows Coryn, Soren, and the others to this faraway place of blue owls, and attacks them . . . Eglantine cut off the thought. She signaled Primrose. "We have to warn them."

"But how? We have no idea how to get there."

"The Palace of Mists!" Eglantine signed. "Soren said if anything happened, we should go and seek Bess at the Palace of Mists."

"We have to get out of here now! We have to warn Soren." Eglantine's wings trembled as she tilted them to signal.

"What about Bell?" Primrose signed back.

"We can't take her back, just the two of us. They're not going to hurt her now. They've got their information. They're going to hold her hostage. She's going to be their bargaining chip, but hopefully we'll be able to get her soon. We'll need to send a message back to the tree."

"Through Gwyndor?"

"Whomever we can get."

Just at that moment they spotted a Great Snowy overhead — a Great Snowy sporting a black feather.

Doc Finebeak!

They took off immediately to tell him what they'd discovered.

Several minutes later, behind a cluster of cactus a
good distance from the rock, Doc Finebeak listened to
Eglantine and Primrose's story. When they had finished,
he blinked and sighed, then plucked the black feather
from his back and broke it in half. "Here, take this, I can
always get another. It will protect you. You're going to
have to fly night and day."

They said a quick good-bye. As the three owls lifted
off in flight, Finebeak heading back to the great tree to
raise troops and Eglantine and Primrose to the Palace of
Mists, they all had one thought: They had beaten the
Pure Ones in the canyonlands in the Battle of Fire and Ice.
They had beaten them in the Beyond. Although this would
not be as big a battle, for the forces would be fewer on
both sides, it could be the most significant battle of all.
The question was not the size of any army. They had to
act now and with great force in a place that was strange
to all of them. Could the Guardians do it again? Never had
so much been at stake — the ember, the king, and an
owlet!

CHAPTER FOURTEEN
The Dragon Court

We treat them like children." Tengshu spoke in a whisper. "They don't know any better. This . . . this way of life, this passivity has been bred into them. It is better this way, believe me."

"They don't mind?" Ruby asked, for what she was seeing was to her mind simply outrageous. Ruby was dumbfounded as she looked on the scene before her. The nine owls were perched on a glistening crystal balcony. Indeed, the entire Panqua Palace of the dragon owls was made from what the sage called geodes — mysterious rocks split open to reveal cavities lined with crystals of luminous colors ranging from pink to sapphire blue to purple and white. Each color was a precious stone with names that the owls had never before heard, like jasper, chalcedony, and agate. The inhabitants of this resplendent, jeweled hollow were known as the dragon owls.

Like Tengshu, their plumage was composed of varying shades of blue. But unlike the sage, they never seemed to have molted. This lack of molting had allowed their feathers to grow to such extraordinary lengths that they swept behind them like cloaks. Flight was impossible. In fact, there were only two ways these owls could travel through air, which was either with assistance from smaller owls who appeared to be servants or with the help of the qui. By hanging on to the string with their talons, they could lift into the air. But if by any chance they were to be separated from their qui, it meant instant death. Their wings were so laden with long heavy feathers they would immediately plummet to the ground. Mostly they walked slowly back and forth across the floor of the palace, with bearers lifting their trains of feathers.

"How did this happen?" Soren said. There was something awful, perverse about seeing owls in this condition. They were dazzlingly beautiful, but their beauty was in such stark contrast to the true nature of owls, or any bird: They could not fly, and despite their splendor, there was something revolting about them.

"It is complicated to explain, but they do not molt naturally."

"But how do they prevent molting?" Otulissa asked. "And why?"

"It is not simply that molting is prevented. That is only part of it. As you know, we owls all have a preen gland at the base of our tails, which provides the oil with which we preen and clean our feathers and that keeps them supple. These particular owls have been cursed with abnormally large preen glands. The extra oil makes their feathers grow faster, but this growth seems to slow actual molting. See how long their tail feathers grow? Quite dazzling, aren't they? It's as if these dragon owls have become transfixed by their own beauty. To maintain it, they are required to stimulate this growth even further by a very complicated method of pruning their undertail coverts. It's almost an unwritten law, a law enforced by their own vanity really, that they do this." Indeed, many of the dragon owls' tail feathers grew to unbelievable lengths.

"Do they like to be this way?" Otulissa asked.

"They don't mind. They accept it. It is part of their phonqua."

"Phonqua?" Digger asked. "What is phonqua?"

The sage shook his head. "It is difficult to explain to owls who are not from our world. It has to do with consequences due to an owl's previous actions, their will for power. They failed to realize that to pursue power only for the sake of power is a transgression against all of nature, beginning with their very own as owls, as creatures of the sky and of the earth. And thus it is a violation of all that Glaux has given us. If one pursues such a course, it skews one's fate. Indeed, they become the victims of power — the power of phonqua."

"You mean this is their fate, their destiny?" Otulissa asked.

Digger felt a quiver in his gizzard. He squinted his eyes. *Consequences due to an owl's previous actions . . . a transgression against all of nature.* The words threaded through his mind. *Could these owls be . . . ? No . . . no.* But Digger observed how their feathers, though beautiful, flowed in ragged streams from their bodies. *Imagine them,* he thought, *as black feathers — not turquoise nor sapphire nor sky nor midnight blue — just glistening black. Could these dragon owls in some past generation have been hagsfiends? And perhaps,* Digger thought, *it is fortunate that they have been made powerless by their very vanity. And would not this pomp and luxury give them the illusion of power?* A shiver went through his gizzard, and he even wilfed a bit, which Tengshu noticed.

"Do not worry, my friend." The sage turned to Digger. "These owls are perfectly harmless. They are listless, dull of wit. But very vain. All they really care about is preening and living in this beautiful palace. They are like poor invalids. I bring them qui and show them how to make their own. But they are easily bored and distracted. Difficult for them to concentrate long enough to finish a task."

None of these words set Digger's mind at ease. *Suppose,* the Burrowing Owl's thoughts continued, *that hagsfiends had come to the Middle Kingdom in the wake of Theo. Could it have been Theo's idea to install them in absolute luxury and distract them with the illusion of power, thus making them essentially harmless? Through some gradual alchemy had their hideous black feathers metamorphosed into this panoply of gorgeous iridescent hues ranging from sea green to turquoise to sapphire?* The sage had spoken of the old court and how useless it had become. Digger recalled Tengshu's words when they first met. *Once we did have a court, but it became useless and, in its uselessness, even dangerous.* So possibly it was Theo who had given the court another use, another function, and at the same time ensured that it would never be a threat. Was this what had been explained in the Theo Papers as part of the way of noble gentleness? Do not kill your enemies; render them impotent through their own delusions of power.

"And now," Tengshu continued. "We must go see the Dowager Empress. It is time for tea. These owls love ceremony and ritual. It fills their nights, passes the time."

"Passes the time to what?" Ruby mumbled.

The flight to the dowager's quarters in Panqua Palace was not a long one. As they approached, Tengshu nodded toward a large opening in a cliff. It appeared from the outside to be a very ordinary-looking cliff, and they expected to fly into a large, very ordinary cave, one such as bats might roost in. But with the first wing beat into the cave such notions were quickly dispelled. Never in their lives had they seen such a dazzling sight. The walls sparkled with threads of glittering rock that wove through patches of exotic stones and crystal formations. "Is this quartz? Mica?" Otulissa wondered aloud. A page with a ten-foot-long train of feathers swept out from what appeared to be a tree entirely composed of pink crystals.

"Welcome to the Hollow of Benevolence and Forgiveness. The Dowager Empress awaits you." The page then sidled up to Tengshu. He spoke in rapid Jouzhen, and although Otulissa tried to pick it up, she only understood a little. Tengshu, however, looked alarmed.

Martin whispered to the others, "I thought everything was always just perfect here — lazy, listless owls. It's suppose to be glaumora. What's the problem?"

"Something about a defection," Otulissa whispered. "And the Dowager Empress is upset."

Tengshu turned to Otulissa. "You're right, and this is most unusual. The empress is eager to meet you because she feels that since you come from the Five Kingdoms you might know something, or have seen something of this errant owl."

"Believe me," Twilight said. "If I had seen a blue owl with such long tail feathers I would have said something by now."

"Well, she's a bit upset. This is not an emotion that she is used to, nor one that these owls handle well."

"Oh, Great Glaux," Gylfie whispered as they approached a throne made of purple chunks of amethyst on which a huge owl with a mixture of cobalt blue and lighter turquoise feathers was perched. Behind her, a special frame held her tail feathers, and to each side were additional frames on which her wings rested. Even her facial-disk feathers were so long that they fell like a screen, veiling her eyes. On her talons, which appeared shriveled and dull, she wore several rings. Her body heaved with sobs.

"Tengshu, he's left! He's left! What will this do to our phonqua?" Otulissa was trying her best to translate this for the rest of the Chaw of Chaws. The empress then turned to the owls. The movement of her feathers caused a wind to stir through the hollow.

"She wants to know if you have seen this owl," Tengshu translated.

"We certainly would have noticed," Coryn said. "Tell her we have not."

Tengshu turned again to her and spoke rapidly, then translated the exchange. "It seems that this owl, Orlando, managed to secretly stop plucking his undertail coverts. A servant was bribed to keep the secret, and then after he had stopped new growth he managed one night to chop off a great quantity of his long tail feathers. A pile was discovered in the Hollow of the Eternal Feathers; this act is considered the gravest of insults. Of course, little can be done now."

"But how could he fly with so little experience?" Ruby asked.

"Poorly, I would imagine," Tengshu said drily. "But if he found the reverse current of the River of Wind . . ."

"And what about that phonqua?" Digger asked. "This . . . this notion of fate and consequences?"

Tengshu looked at him darkly. He began to speak and then hesitated. "I . . . I don't think that one dragon owl's actions could disturb the phonqua of our entire kingdom. It would not seem fair, would it?" He spoke with a forced cheerfulness.

Digger blinked and waited to speak. "Nor would it seem fair for it to disturb the phonqua of our five kingdoms. But some say that the flutterings of one butterfly can disturb the universe."

"Yes, it's a part of weather theory," Otulissa began, "discovered by a very distinguished relative of mine, the renowned weathertrix, Strix Emerilla."

"I was speaking of this, Otulissa, in a more philosophical sense," Digger interrupted. "The notion that the smallest variations of what philosophers call the initial condition might produce large variations in the long-term behavior of the system."

The Dowager Empress was poking at Tengshu with her scepter while she studied Digger. It was obvious that she wanted to know what he was saying.

"This will indeed *disturb* the empress unnecessarily, I fear," Tengshu said, and then turned to the empress and spoke some Jouzhen that none of them understood. But they did hear the word "phonqua." From the manner in which she settled back on her throne, they assumed that Tengshu had assuaged her fears concerning phonqua and the fate of the owls of the Dragon Court. But there were others who were not so relieved, in particular Digger and Mrs. Plithiver.

No words needed to be spoken between the Burrowing Owl and the blind snake. They both sensed that something greater was at stake than the peace of mind of the empress.

CHAPTER FIFTEEN

The Butterfly that Disturbs

M rs. P.," Digger started suddenly. He had been in deep thought in the crystal cocoonlike cavity that he had been shown to in the Panqua Palace.

"I didn't mean to disturb you, dear."

"I couldn't sleep. Don't worry about it."

"I know," Mrs. Plithiver replied.

Digger blinked. "You do?"

"Well, I know that something is disturbing you and that sleep would be hard to come by."

At that moment, Gylfie flew in from a connecting cave. "You can't sleep, either?" Digger asked.

"No." She shook her head. "I think Martin is up, too." Within two minutes, all eight owls had crammed into the cavity with Digger. They all seemed agitated.

"It's this phonqua business, isn't it?" Mrs. P. said.

"It's very weird — the phonqua, this whole place," Martin said.

"And it's not just that," Soren added. "I'm worried about this defector."

"Yes, the defector," Digger said in a hesitant voice, and then he seemed to gather strength. He was suddenly happy that he could share these feelings and the frightening thoughts he had had when the sage first told them all about the dragon owls. "The dragon owls appear weak, vain, ridiculous, and powerless. But how did they come to be this way?" He swiveled his head slowly, searching each owl's face for an answer. But none was forthcoming. "What have they done to earn this life, which is hardly a life?"

"And yet it makes the rest of the owls of this sixth kingdom safe from them," Otulissa said. "Assuming, of course, that they had previously been brutal or evil owls."

Then Soren very tentatively took a step toward Digger. "Are you imagining these owls in another . . . another . . ." He searched for a word. ". . . guise, Digger?"

Digger could scarcely breathe. "I must be honest." He shut his eyes. *Just say it. Just say it*, he told himself silently. "I have had thoughts of hagsfiends." There was a gasp from the owls.

"What kinds of thoughts?" Soren asked.

Digger took a deep breath and began to speak slowly.

"I began to think about hagsfiends when Tengshu spoke of phonqua, their fate. They accept this pathetic excuse for a real owl's life because they are paying a debt in hopes of redeeming themselves. But something has gone wrong with this defector. He has desires. A will that is alien to his nature, to his phonqua, and the others are now fearful that it has skewed everything."

"Yes, the butterfly that disturbed the universe," Mrs. P. replied softly.

"What's to be done?" Digger asked.

"It is not our fate to deal with. Not our world." Mrs. P. said.

"But what if he goes to *our* world? What then?"

"I don't know, Digger. I honestly don't know." Mrs. P. sighed, then coiled up and swung her head toward the owls. "We cannot solve any of this right now. So all of you go back to your day nests in those cavities and try to get some sleep."

"I don't know how one is supposed to sleep in all that glittery rock," Ruby muttered. "The whole place just buzzes with too many colors."

Digger turned and looked at Ruby. "You're right. This is the most resplendent place I have ever been to. It is what I once might have imagined to be glaumora, but it is truly hagsmire, Ruby. Truly hagsmire."

I have to go back! Now. I have to go back. I'll find the Zong Phong. She's in danger ... I know it. Before they could stop him he was off, and suddenly he was back in his own world on the familiar side of the Unnamed Sea. But he had landed, oddly enough, in Kuneer. The hot desert thermals were rising. She was trapped beneath the sand, young, little, and vulnerable. A blue feather floated up in the desert air. Soren shreed, *"I will help you ... I promise ... if it's the last thing I do ... I will help you."*

"Wake up! Soren! Wake up!" Twilight and Ruby were both shaking him fiercely. "It's just a bad dream."

"Starsight? Here?" Gylfie asked. "Even with all the constellations being different?"

"It was so real," Soren said, shaking his head. "Someone is in trouble ... I can't remember who, though. I think we have to go back."

Starsight was a phenomenon in which the stars in the sky in some mysterious way illuminated Soren's dreams. Most creatures thought that during the day, when nocturnal animals slept, the stars vanished, but for some they did not. The stars became little holes in the fabric of their dreams, and through these holes they saw things happening far away, or in the future, things that often came true.

"I just have this terrible feeling in my gizzard."

"I do, too," Digger said.

"Do you think we should go back?" Soren asked.

Digger shook his head. "No. I am afraid I feel quite the opposite. I think it is imperative that we stay. Stay and figure things out."

"Do you think we are in danger of some sort from this new world?" Coryn asked.

"Not exactly. I mean, I think we have been brought here as a part our phonqua. I truly believe that Tengshu is a good owl."

"*Our* phonqua?" Otulissa asked.

"I think, in fact, Otulissa, that the universe is about to be disturbed," Digger replied.

"A butterfly?" Gylfie asked.

"No, a dragon owl."

"Huh?" Ruby said.

At that moment, there was a noise outside the hollow where Soren had been sleeping. A long, low hoot was heard and Tengshu alighted. "The Dowager Empress's qui bearers are coming. She wants to meet with you. She's in a very agitated state. You can't imagine. She rarely leaves the Hollow of Benevolence and Forgiveness. She will be here any second."

The owls of Ga'Hoole came out of the hollow into the wide passage that was lined with rich purple crystals of jasper. It was a stunning sight to see this immense owl towed by a qui. Her wings and tail feathers spread across a frame suspended from the superstructure of silk cloth and paper. There were perhaps a half-dozen bearers, normally feathered owls handling the strings. Various instructions were being called out that guided the operations of the strings to control the qui. She did not really fly, but hovered a few inches above the floor of the palace. As the strings were reeled in, the qui floated down and so did the empress. Her body was heaving with sobs. She called Tengshu to her side and began speaking rapidly. He held up a talon to halt this rush of words, then turned to Coryn.

"I must translate for the empress. She urgently wants you to understand this unfortunate, nay, tragic situation that has occurred with the defection of the owl known as Orlando." There was another rush of words from the empress. "She feels that this defection has twisted the phonqua of the dragon owls of the Panqua Palace." Tengshu began to stammer a bit and it was apparent that he was reluctant to go on. He and the Dowager Empress exchanged glances. There were some desperate whisperings between them. Tengshu then turned to the owls of Ga'Hoole. "There are some things that, though shared between our cultures, have diverged and taken different paths. These things cannot really be explained."

Cannot or will not? Soren wondered.

"The dragon owls here in the Panqua Palace are servants . . ."

Servants! The word exploded silently in the heads of all of the owls of Ga'Hoole. These owls served nothing. They existed only to be served. They could not even fly on their own. The notion of them serving others was absolutely preposterous.

"But what are we supposed to do?" Digger asked.

"How can we help?" Coryn stepped forward. "You speak of twisting the phonqua, but we hardly understand the meaning of this word, let alone what your phonqua is."

"You must go to the owlery. A messenger has already been sent to the first master of the pikyus, requesting an audience for you with the H'ryth."

Otulissa blinked. "What did you say?"

"The H'ryth," Tengshu repeated. "It is the holy one of the owlery. That is what we call him, the H'ryth. He must be consulted on all matters of phonqua."

"Yes, of course," said Otulissa, and clamped her beak shut. The owls of Ga'Hoole swiveled their heads toward her. This sudden silence was not normal behavior for Otulissa. She was usually more than ready to share her thoughts, her opinions. Digger looked at her thoughtfully. *What is she not saying?*

The Dowager Empress was departing now with her cadre of bearers. The wind in the amethyst corridor stirred as she was borne back a few inches above the palace floor on her qui to the Hollow of Benevolence and Forgiveness, but within this wind, Mrs. Plithiver detected a tinier riffle of a breeze. It was as if the wings of a butterfly had stirred the air. The universe was about to be disturbed.

CHAPTER SIXTEEN

The Desert Healer

Far away in the Desert of Kuneer, an Elf Owl poked his head from the cavity in the cactus. He saw the moonfaced owl and a small division of her followers flying overhead in a westerly direction. *Good!* he thought. *They're gone. Now I can get to work.* Eglantine and Primrose had not been the only owls listening that night to the voices that had filtered up though Nyra's burrow. Cuffyn the desert healer had also been listening, but from another place.

The Elf Owl was prodigiously intelligent. Not only was he a fine and esteemed herbalist and healer, he had learned the ways of the Burrowing Owls, who were numerous in the Desert of Kuneer, and despite his small size, he had become an excellent excavator and digger of tunnels, very small tunnels that were nearly undetectable. He had become deeply suspect of these Barn Owls who had arrived in Kuneer and seemed to be growing in numbers with each passing cycle of the moon. He harbored a particular resentment for the one called Stryker. That brute had roughed him up to obtain some of his precious gizzard tonic. Shortly after that, he began his surveillance activities and had made the exquisite network of tunnels that led to the central burrow of these Barn Owls. He had taken to the tunnels two nights before when he saw yet another small Barn Owl being flown in. Owl-napping, that's what they were up to! Cuffyn was convinced of this. Shortly after that, he saw the strangest sight of all — a large blue owl being air-dragged to the central hollow. He quickly took to his tunnels and made his way toward the central burrow to listen in.

While Eglantine and Primrose had taken off at the first mention of Nyra's plan to go to the strange world to follow the Chaw of Chaws, Cuffyn had stayed on and heard the agonizing cries of the blue owl as they attempted to extract additional information from him, and then heard his dazed ramblings as they forced a serum upon him. Cuffyn blinked. *Racdrops! They stole that from me! How did they know about it? These owls are beyond belief!* He listened carefully as the blue owl spoke in a slow, slurred voice.

"At the farthest edge to the north in the land of volcanoes, you must go to the place where the water from the sea of vastness swirls into an inlet. Fly there, for that is the only way to the Zong Phong — which will take you to the Middle Kingdom. But it is hard to find. When you leave the coast behind, fly due west out to sea, to tomorrow, and then find the windkins to the Zong Phong. . . . To tomorrow, that is the first part of the journey."

"What do you mean — to tomorrow?" Nyra rasped.

"To tomorrow. You'll know . . . you'll know. There is a hole in the wind. . . . when day turns to black . . . the death of day . . . then up the windkins and into the central trough of this river of air. It will swiftly take you to the other side. Then down, down, down the windkins to the other side. Follow the qui lines of the sage. They will lead you down . . . down . . . down. . . ."

The drugged ramblings of the blue owl raised more questions than they answered. But once again Sergeant Tarn proved himself of invaluable service. He fetched a rather tattered map of the Beyond that he had kept from his days as a hireclaw seeking Rogue smiths who made weapons in the land of volcanoes.

"I think he means to go here." The Burrowing Owl pointed his talon at a region north of the volcanoes.

"But there is nothing there," Nyra said.

"It doesn't show on the map because it is far from the volcanoes where the Rogue smiths set their forges. It's just barren to the north, few ever fly there. But the vast sea scrapes the edges. I think this is where we will find the inlet he speaks of."

"But what about this flying to tomorrow?" Stryker asked.

"That I am not sure of," Tarn said.

"And the windkins?" Nyra asked.

"They must lead to this very swift current, I would guess a very high-altitude wind."

"Get set to fly before the moon rises," Nyra barked at her owls. "And let me make one thing perfectly clear: This mission is a slink melf. That means we go in not with a division or a regiment — not even a platoon or a squadron. We go in light, armed but low in the number of owls. This is an assassination — the targets are the so-called king and his uncle. They are our immediate goals. There are not many Guardians — just the Chaw of Chaws. Our scouts saw them heading across the Beyond on a northwest course. Now we know for sure. An entire division of owls flying over Kuneer, through Ambala, and all the way to the Beyond will rouse suspicion. We do not want to rouse suspicion. Understood?"

"Yes, General Mam."

"We will fly with eighteen owls including yourselves." She nodded at Wort, Stryker, and Tarn. "And one other thing." She looked directly at Lieutenant Stryker as she spoke. "I would like to announce a promotion." Stryker swelled up with excitement. "I am promoting Sergeant Tarn to Captain."

"What?" Stryker gasped.

"You have a problem with that, Stryker?"

"Uh . . . no . . . uh . . . b-b-but . . ."

"But what?"

"Nothing, General Mam."

"Oh, one other thing." She paused and looked at the officers gathered around her. "The owl who kills Soren, or the king, will win an immediate promotion to adjunct general."

There was a gasp among the owls. Not since the time of Kludd had there been an adjunct general, and at that time the AG had been Nyra herself. In Nyra's mind, there was more than just the death of these two owls at stake. With them gone, the Band would weaken, and when the Band weakened, the Chaw of Chaws weakened, and when the Chaw of Chaws weakened, the Great Ga'Hoole Tree would be vulnerable, and the way to the ember, the powerful Ember of Hoole would be clear. It was the ember she wanted, that she lusted for. With it, all the kingdoms of owls would be hers.

The owls wasted no time. They flew off immediately

and left a light guard behind with the blue owl and the little Barn Owl.

Cuffyn blinked as he listened to all this. The brutality of these owls, their evil, knew no bounds. Well, he was a healer, not a fighter. His life had been dedicated to helping the weak through the herbal arts. And he was determined to help this strange blue owl and the little owlet. He would not countenance owl-napping. He did not dare open flight right now, but returned through the network of tunnels to his cactus. *Bingle juice*, he thought, *laced with a heavy sleeping draft. That'll do it.* He knew these owls drank spirits when the top lieutenants were away, especially the old one called Ifghar and his snake, Gragg. They were loyal to this moonfaced owl mostly out of fear, but discipline lapsed when she was away with her high-ranking officers. They were small of gizzard, the lot of them, and had no imagination. Cuffyn might be a quarter their size, but he could outwit them, and that was exactly what he planned to do. *Desert trash, the lot of them!*

The blue owl blinked his eyes open. "Striga, are you all right?" Bell asked.

"What did I say? What did I say?" he asked urgently, though his voice was shaky.

"Oh, nothing much. I mean it was kind of hard to understand. Something about flying west. I think you meant to the Beyond and the Unnamed Sea and finding a hole in the wind."

"I said that? I said all that?!"

"Yeah, but it sounded like nonsense. You know, like it really didn't mean anything."

"But it does," he said frantically. "It does."

"Hey, shut up in there." A Sooty Owl stuck his head in. "You want another whack?" Bell cowered in the corner. The blue owl wilfed, then slowly swiveled his head toward Bell. *How could I be so weak? How could I have said all that?* And then feeling a deep twinge in his gizzard, he thought, *And how could I have let this dear little owl down? I want to save something. I know it is my phonqua to save something. I am a good owl. I am a good owl. . . .*

He turned toward Bell and blinked. "Come here, little one. These desert nights are cold, aren't they? Tuck under my wing."

Bell nestled under the blue wing. "Your feathers are so long. Don't you ever molt?"

"Very seldom. They just keep growing."

"No wonder you have so much trouble flying."

"Yes, it is a . . . a . . ." He searched for the right word.

"We call it a wingicap." Bell yawned.

"That's a good word, yes, a wingicap. But I'm going to grow stronger. You'll see."

"How did you ever fly all the way here from the Northern Kingdoms?"

"Very favorable winds — very favorable."

It wasn't quite a lie, but the blue owl did not feel good about what he had just said.

Eglantine and Primrose, following Soren's instructions, had sought out Bess. Now, deep in the Shadow Forest where the trees dipped steeply behind the gossamer spray of the great waterfalls, they huddled with the Boreal Owl over some very ancient-looking charts in the library of the Palace of Mists.

"I so regret," Bess was saying, "that I had not completed these calculations when your brother and the others left for the Middle Kingdom. For a long time after they left, I just had some . . . how should I call it? Some vague inklings about these windkins. They are more treacherous than I had originally thought, with very deadly wind shears. You must avoid these tumblebones that can pop up unexpectedly in the midst of a windkin. Now you understand the key and its symbols, but these symbols cannot tell you everything." Through finding further documents, Bess had discovered evidence of the same phenomenon that Mrs. P. had sensed. When explaining it to Eglantine and Primrose, she even used words similar to those of Mrs. Plithiver. "You see," she said, "I believe that central stream of air — think of it as a river of wind — begins to influence time, perhaps because it carries us so fast, to where a new night, a new day begins." Then, with words so identical to Mrs. Plithiver's as to be astonishing, Bess said, "Look, the earth is round. Here, it is day right now. On the other side of the earth it must be night. The sun cannot be every-place at once. Tomorrow has to start somewhere, and I think it begins out there, far over the Unnamed Sea. It all makes so much sense now. The way into the windkin is easy if you can find this point. And if you start now, you'll be well ahead of Nyra." She smoothed the chart with one talon and set down the key, then began tracing a path. "Due west. I think if my calculations are right, there will be sudden blackness and then you will be blown into tomorrow."

Blown into tomorrow? Whatever did that mean? both Eglantine and Primrose wondered. "You have the crow feather. It's broad daylight but you'll be safe to fly now. You should go immediately."

"What do you want?" Bell jerked awake. Someone was outside the burrow. She nudged the blue owl. "Striga, someone's out there. Not one of those Pure Ones. Someone else," she whispered.

It was a new voice. One they had not heard before. "Your commander, General Mam, sent for these potions. Tonic for her gizzard. She's been taking it for a moon cycle now. It goes down best with some bingle juice. So I brought some of that as well. But of course the bingle juice doesn't keep that long. I'd hate to have to fly all the way back with it."

"Well, she won't be long. We'll take care of it until she returns," one of the guards answered.

I am sure you will, thought Cuffyn as he handed over the pouch of bingle juice that he had laced with a powerful sleeping draft. *I am sure you will, idiot owls!*

CHAPTER SEVENTEEN

The Owlery at the Mountain of Time

O tulissa ruminated, *What of this owl who now leads us, this three-hundred-year-old owl who is flying almost as strongly as Ruby, whose mother had traveled to our kingdom, perhaps in the time of Theo?* It was all so mystifying. Tengshu had said that the owlery was located in the Mountain of Time. He had explained that it was also called the Hollow Mountain, as the word "time" and "hollow" in their language were one and the same — hulong. There was no Krakish word that even vaguely resembled it.

Blades of moonlight stabbed through the clouds, illuminating rank upon rank of icy peaks ahead. From the ground, however, there was a sudden swirl of the smell that they had learned to associate with the lamps that these owls burned in their hollows. "It's a buttery below!" Tengshu called back. "The yaks gather to yield their milk that pikyus churn into butter."

Soren swiveled his head toward Twilight, who was flying next to him. "Amazing!"

"I'd like to bring some back," said Gylfie, who was flying in Twilight's wake for protection against the strong icy gusts.

"Are you yoicks?!" Twilight said. "It stinks!"

"I'm getting used to it," Gylfie replied. "You have to get a little more adventurous in your taste."

"I don't want to taste it."

"You know what I mean."

"You don't call this adventurous? Flying behind a three-hundred-and-twenty-five-year-old blue owl — from a jeweled palace full of dragon owls who can't fly — to this 'owlery' to consult with a whatever they call it — you don't call this adventurous?" Twilight spoke with exaggerated wonder drenching his every word.

"H'ryth," Otulissa broke in. "I just figured it out."

"Figured what out?" asked Martin, who was flying under Otulissa's port wing for protection.

"The word. What it means."

"Yeah?" said Twilight. "So, what does it mean?"

"Innermost part of the gizzard in old Krakish. These owls' connections with the Northern Kingdoms are much greater than we ever imagined," Otulissa said.

The wind was now shrieking through a corrugated

landscape of ice cliffs and spires, not dissimilar from parts of the Northern Kingdoms, especially before the time of the first Great Melt, which was a period just after the era of the legends. At that time, a warm maverick wind from the south had blown for moon cycle after moon cycle, year after year, and the vast glaciers and towering icy peaks had begun to dissolve. But now as they flew, they could feel a wind snaking through narrow valleys, piling up amid ice and rock ridges and escarpments, creating a violent high-pressure strata of air in which their flight became quite tumultuous.

"Be careful here!" Tengshu called out.

"Careful!" Ruby said. She, however, was mad for this air and was flying like an owl possessed.

"Get back into formation, Ruby," Coryn barked. "This isn't a game of scooters." Scooters were land breezes that spilled off the edges of the island of Hoole at certain times of the year and provided great sport for its owls.

A sudden loud boom rang out. Soren felt his ear slits contract against the sound. The noise shook all the owls right down to their pinfeathers and reverberated throughout their hollow bones.

"Don't worry!" Tengshu shouted. "It's just the wind bong."

"Wind bong?" Martin asked, still shaking.

"In our language it translates to 'last shriek of a mighty wind.' It bursts through that notch directly below us and then is free again."

A high plain now rose beneath them. At its far edge, ranks of peaks rose even higher than the ones they had just left behind. These peaks cut the sky like the teeth of a serrated knife. The air was so clear, they could immediately pick out in the far distance owls rising in the night, and above them colorful qui danced in the shafts of moonlight.

"They can fly, can't they?" Ruby asked.

"Oh, yes. Those are prayer qui. It is the third hour of the death of day and the first quarter of the hatch of night, so they offer the prayers to the wind gods and the ones of night hatch."

"Night hatch? Wind gods?" Soren asked. "Are they like Glaux?"

"Oh, they are all Glaux. In our language, we call them the khyre of Glaux. Which means . . ."

"'The many faces of Glaux,' in old Krakish," Otulissa whispered to herself. *What in the world awaits us?*

A gong thundered through the mountain passes as the owls landed on a platform of the owlery outside a cavelike opening in the mountain. A group of what

Tengshu called pikyus had flown out to greet them. These owls could not have been more different from those of the Panqua Palace. Their plumage was tightly clipped, and the top of their heads nearly bare except for one bright blue feather that stuck straight up.

"I don't see how they can even fly," Gylfie whispered to Soren. But they did, and without any aid from the qui. It was obvious that they flew the qui and not the reverse — the qui definitely did not fly them. The pikyus all stood now with their qui beside them. They came up and first bowed deeply to Tengshu.

One pikyu, who except for his blue color resembled a Boreal Owl, stepped forward. "Hee naow, qui dong Tengshu."

"He's welcoming Tengshu, the knower of qui," Otulissa whispered. The pikyu then turned to the owls of Ga'Hoole, bowed, and welcomed them as honored guests. He indicated that they were to follow him.

"We now go see the H'ryth." They entered the mountain. Everything was completely different from the resplendent jeweled hollows of the Panqua Palace. There were no luminous colors, and the only crystals were those formed by the ice. But because of the large torches of yak butter, much of the interior had melted down to reveal lovely gray stone swirled with streaks of white quartz.

The owls flew through long, twisting corridors in an ascending spiral. Other corridors meandered off the central one, and it was clear that within the Hollow Mountain, or Mountain of Time as they called it, there was a bustling community. But it seemed quieter than most communities of owls. It was understandable that this place would be called the Hollow Mountain — but why a Mountain of Time? Was it because the lives of the owls who lived here stretched across so many centuries that the mountain itself was thought to be a receptacle of time? There were perch-loads of chanting owls. Surrounding them, the qui painted with the various gods or faces of Glaux hung. *More like a mountain of prayer than a mountain of time,* Soren thought as they flew through the vast caverns that formed the interior of the mountain.

They finally reached the highest point. Above them, portals opened, through which they could see streaming clouds driven by incredibly fierce winds. They were directed to settle on a perch that appeared to be as hard as the rock around them. "It's not rock," Otulissa whispered. "It's petrified wood. Millions of years old, I think." Another gong sounded. A small pikyu flew forward and in very good Hoolian but with a definite Krakish accent began to speak.

"Welcome," he said. "I present His Holiness, Gup

Theosang, the seventh H'ryth of the Owlery of the Mountain of Time."

At that moment, a pale blue owl flew forward. He looked no different from any of the rest of the pikyus except that from his eyes streamed a pale greenish light. "It is," whispered Tengshu, "the gleam of deep wisdom. It comes from a life of complete dedication to the basic values of owlness. You might detect subtle glints of green in some of our eyes, but none as vivid this."

"Theosang?" Otulissa whispered.

"It comes from the name of our first H'ryth — Theo," Tengshu replied.

Theo! The name hung in the air like the echo of a chime, a chime in the Mountain of Time.

CHAPTER EIGHTEEN
A Feather in the Wind

Look! Look over there at those ... those ... those ... It looks like something from the weavers guild at the great tree. Something torn loose from the loom," Primrose shouted.

This must be a sign that we're getting nearer to something, Eglantine thought. If it were true, she would be glad. Although the long flight on the River of Wind in many ways had not been as arduous as she had expected, she knew that the terrible sight of those mummified creatures spinning through the tumblebones would haunt her for a long time. She had felt compelled to look at them, for she was fearful that her own brother or some other Chaw of Chaw member might have been caught in them. So despite the lovely, soft, swift breezes of the River of Wind, she had never been able to completely relax. And she was still uncertain if Soren, the king, and the rest of the Chaw of Chaws had actually arrived on this side of the Unnamed Sea.

She looked up in the direction that Primrose had indicated. Something colorful was dancing in the wind eddies of this marvelous stream of air that had borne them across the Unnamed Sea. They began to follow the strings of the qui just as the Chaw of Chaws had done a few nights before. But this time, the welcoming gong did not sound. Tengshu, who had returned to his hollow at the end of the River of Wind, was caught completely by surprise. He looked up, startled from minding his qui.

"Hee naow, hee naow," the sage stammered. "I . . . I was not expecting you. . . . You are Soren's sister?" The similarity was striking. But Primrose and Eglantine were blinking in amazement. The color of this owl was astonishing, and yet had they not seen blue feathers in Ambala? And now this blue owl was talking about her brother. *My brother! Soren!*

Eglantine gasped with relief. "You mean they got here?"

"Oh, yes, yes! Soren-sister and Little One." The sage nodded toward Primrose.

"Thank Glaux!" Eglantine and Primrose said at once. "We must find them immediately," Eglantine said. Her voice was almost hoarse with desperation. "The Pure Ones — they are coming. A slink melf — an assassination squad."

So this was it, thought the sage. This was the undecipherable part of the eight astrologers' prediction that had been written in an ancient form of Krakish. There were suggestions of some threat that was to come. But who would have ever thought so soon? When he had returned from the owlery, he had left the Spotted Owl, the one called Otulissa, pondering the writings of the eight astrologers. Tengshu knew that action was necessary, not further thought. He must dispatch these owls to the owlery with all haste and stay here to "welcome" the vicious owls that were to follow.

"You must fly, Soren-sister, to that distant ridge and then to the next that will appear. Keep Little One," he said, nodding at Primrose, "under wing, for the winds turn very boisterous."

"But Eglantine," Primrose said. "You've lost your crow feather."

"Crow feather?" the sage asked.

"Crow feathers protect us from crows during daylight, and it's almost day now."

"There are no crows here. Do not worry. Just go. And take this." Tengshu tore off the red tail of his qui. "Fly with this. It is the signal for danger. Imminent danger! Now fly!"

*   *   *

Far behind them, across that vast sea, a black feather drifted in lazy swirls.

"What's this?" the Burrowing Owl Tarn asked.

"What's what?" Nyra barked. The frinking blue owl's instructions had got them absolutely nowhere. "Zong Phong . . . fly to tomorrow," she muttered.

"It looks like part of the crow feather that Doc Finebeak flies with," Stryker said.

"What?" A new heat surged through Nyra's somewhat restored gizzard. "Finebeak! The traitor!" The Snowy, the finest tracker in any kingdom, had joined the owls of the great tree. He had once tracked down her own son. Nyra flew to where Tarn and Stryker were hovering. She stared at the feather and blinked in disbelief. *What luck!* "This must be the way. The Guardians have gone this way. Follow me!"

Nyra started a banking turn and examined the center of the swirl where the black feather rotated. They followed it up and suddenly were caught in a savage crosscurrent of slashing winds. The rest of the Pure Ones had followed their General Mam, the supreme commander of the Tytonic Union of Pure Ones. But they now seemed to be fighting for their lives. Nyra ducked in and out of the rungs of the ladder of confusing windkins. "Follow me!"

she cried. Tarn was right on her tail, as were Stryker and Wort, but two Barn Owls were sucked away and a Sooty was fighting to escape the grip of the tumblebones. His dark eyes froze in fear first as he saw the feathers stripped from his wing, and then with the terrible realization that his port wing was separating from his body.

But, finally, the rest of the Pure Ones were safe at last in the streaming River of Wind. Nyra looked around. Yes, she had lost three officers of the slink melf, but there were fifteen others, including Tarn, thank Glaux, who had survived. "We're here!" Nyra screamed triumphantly as she tumbled into the racing currents of the Zong Phong. "We're on their track. Vengeance is ours!"

Tengshu had sharpened his talons on his flintstone. He knew about battle claws, but there was not a pair to be found in the Middle Kingdom. They were forbidden, and had been ever since the time of the first H'ryth, Theosang, who was the battle claw inventor and had left that world of warring owls behind. If owls needed to fight and to kill they would have to find other ways. This was considered the most sacred proscription of any H'ryth in the history of the Middle Kingdom. But fighting is an instinct among all animals, and often a necessity, although the owls of the Middle Kingdom seldom admitted such, for even that seemed like a violation of the great first H'ryth's philosophy. Compared to other owls, these blue ones were quite peaceful. But they had, over the centuries, developed skills that were every bit as effective as battle claws. And as Tengshu squinted into the dawn and saw his prayer qui torn from the sky, he hardened his gizzard and realized that for the first time in a century, he was about to use these skills.

The sun glinted off the battle claws of the Pure Ones. These owls were armed, but that didn't bother Tengshu. It was to his advantage. He could fly better, faster, more nimbly, without the additional weight.

"Eeeyrrrrk!" he screeched, and like a blue bolt of lightning he cracked the noon stillness with his cry. It was not a battle cry, but one that was known as the "zong qui," literally the breath of the qui, which would expand an owl's lungs, and when expelled thrust him through the air at blinding speed. Tengshu had been schooled in the fine art of Danyar, the way of noble gentleness. The exercises he had learned those many years ago, which he continued to practice, had one purpose: to develop the entire owl organism — joints, hollow bones, gizzard, lungs, heart, and feathers — so that an owl could strike with great force using every part and fiber of its body. Tengshu repeated the chant of the Danyar. "I am the root of the tree, the breath of the dragon, the clearness of the air, and the brightness of the stars in the pitch of the night." He could feel the huge wind, the breath of qui, flow through him.

"What is it?" Stryker gasped as he saw the blue streak hurtling toward him. In the next second, he had been rendered senseless by a blow to his chest. He plummeted unconscious to the ground. There was blood, but it was caused by the rock he lay impaled upon. Danyar was not about spilling blood, but depriving another of their senses, rendering them unconscious. If they were killed or torn apart, it was rarely from the sharpened talons. To tear with talons was considered an undisciplined way to win combat. Although the end result might be the same — death — the less bloodshed the better. Three more Pure Ones fell from the sky, not from a blow but from witnessing what had just transpired. Their wings locked and their gizzards turned to stone: They had simply gone yeep.

Nyra felt a terrible unease in her gizzard. Was it one owl that was doing this or several? She peeled off in flight. Tengshu, meanwhile, was engaged with three other Pure Ones. Time for the Zi Phan, the talon like the spiked flower. It was a deadly move, and the three owls followed their lieutenant to the ground.

Tengshu felt the first weakening in his zi field, which was the region of concentrated energy and control. He had done well. The group of a dozen or more owls that the great moonfaced owl had been leading were scattered. They would undoubtedly reunite, but he had slowed them down. Still, he was three hundred and twenty-five, he reminded himself — and for that age, he had done a decent job. Hopefully, Soren-sister and Little One had reached the outer winds of the Mountain of Time by now.

Hopefully, he thought, and flew back to his hollow. Some yak tea would restore him and yes, of course, a poem. He must put quill to paper and write — write of something peaceful with great dignity. Isn't that what Theosang had always done?

In the dimness of his hollow wrapped in the rich glow of the butter lamp, he picked up his quill and began to write.

> *Soon it will be spring*
> *Ice melts*
> *The Puoy bird will whoop and wipe its muddy feet on a leaf*
> *A bud begins to unlock its secret*

CHAPTER NINETEEN
A Cycle Broken?

Listen to them." The blue owl spoke softly. "Their words grow thick. They are drinking the bingle juice. You say it will make them drunk?"

"Very," Bell whispered. "My parents only give us just a drop mixed with lots of water on special occasions. But . . . but . . ." Bell cocked her head. The little one was obviously hearing something, the blue owl thought. Her hearing was quite amazing. "I don't think they are drunk yet. But their heartbeats are slowing and they might fall asleep soon. Their breath is snory."

"Asleep? Oh," the blue owl said, suddenly remembering. This was a new word for him.

"Sleep, you know," Bell said, turning to look at him. "What do you call it? Is it different in Krakish?"

"Yes, we call it something else."

"What?"

"We call it going to the spirit realm."

"Oh," Bell said with wonder. "That's nice. I like that. But do you actually go someplace?"

"In a sense."

"Where? Is it a good place?"

"Sometimes it is good, sometimes it is bad."

"Explain it to me."

"It's as if part of us leaves our body as it needs rest . . . the spirit part."

"Sort of like a scroom," Bell said.

"Yes, of course, sort of like a scroom." But the blue owl had no idea what a scroom was. Another little, but not quite, lie.

"And what does your spirit do?"

"It roams."

"Where?"

"It is hard to explain." The blue owl truly did not want to explain. His spirit sometimes roamed to a dark and horrible place. A place he felt he had been before, where his feathers had not been blue, but raggedy and black. A place in which he had been possessed by uncontrollable urges for which he knew he must now pay until the phonqua was completed.

But almost as bad as his previous life was the one he had been forced to lead in the Dragon Court of the Panqua

Palace. A life of complete and utter luxury, a life of no physical need, but a life that was no life at all. It had been severed from what the owls of the Middle Kingdom called the golden thread, which tied the spirit and the body together in a meaningful way. So with the cutting of the golden thread, life became a mockery. Perhaps the worst part was the sheer boredom and the constant shame at the travesty that they had grown to look like the magnificent dragons of the past but had none of their power. Every minute of every night and every moon cycle for year upon year reminded them of their impotence, reminded them of the travesty of their so-called lives in this court.

It was only after years and years that the phonqua could be brought to a close that would result in a new life. He desperately wanted the phonqua fulfilled, the cycle to end, but he was impatient. It was this impatience that had driven him to escape the Panqua Palace. He felt that there must be another way. And now he was going to shorten that cycle. He was going to rescue this little owl. He would restore her to her parents, to this tree they called the Great Ga'Hoole Tree. The guards were asleep, gone to the spirit realm. He was sure he could do it. He had felt himself growing stronger.

So lost in thought was he that he had not noticed that

Bell had crept up the short tunnel to the opening in the burrow where the guards kept their watch. She returned now.

"They're asleep! Sound asleep. We can escape!"

"Escape!" the blue owl said.

"Yes, Striga, escape!"

A few minutes later, they emerged from the desert burrow into the light of the newing moon. It had grown much fatter since they had first arrived in the Desert of Kuneer. It felt good to spread their wings after the tight confines of the tunnel spaces of the underground burrow. The breeze stirred their facial disk feathers, and Bell tipped hers toward the velvety darkness of the sky. "Stars, wind," she whispered softly to herself, and wondered how one could bear to live underground.

"I thought I was going to have to go in there and drag you out." It was an Elf Owl, the same voice that they had heard offering the bingle juice to the guards. "Come on, follow me. Let's get out of here. I have to get you to somewhere safe from these terrible owls."

"Are you sure it's safe to go?" the blue owl asked.

"Yes, the top command is gone. The other owls around here have no idea that you are prisoners. Follow me."

"He can't fly too well," Bell said.

"No, no. I'll be fine," the blue owl assured them both.

Cuffyn looked at him and wondered. What in the name of Glaux had this owl eaten or drunk to make him blue and weak of wing? No time to inquire. They had to get out — now.

"Where will you take me?" Bell asked the Elf Owl. "I want to go home."

"First, let's just get you to safety, and then we'll figure out the rest," the Elf Owl replied. "We don't want this old sot of a snake to wake up before we're out of here."

Bell looked down. She saw the fat old snake, the one she had heard called Gragg. She had to resist yarping a pellet on him for fear of waking him up. There was something about that snake she absolutely hated. He seemed so different from any nest-maid snake. He had given Bell a hard whack when she had first arrived. Apparently, she had not moved down the tunnel quickly enough. And he had called her a really disgusting name — seagull splat.

Oh, Bell could hardly believe it. She was going home . . . home . . . home to the great tree! Home to see her mum, her da, her two sisters, her auntie Plonk and her auntie Ot, for that was what the three B's called Otulissa. Then she remembered, Twilight had promised to give her her first battle claws lesson. And Bubo. *Oh, my! How I have missed Bubo!* What did she want to do first? Curl up in the hollow with Mum and Da and hear stories or go drink milkberry tea with Bubo? *Oh, be with Mum and Da, of course.* They flew on, hours passing like minutes while happy anticpation warmed Bell's gizzard.

Suddenly, she noticed how well the blue owl was flying. "Hey, you're doing great. How did you learn so fast?"

"I'm not sure . . ." the blue owl answered honestly.

Then Bell saw something that made her gizzard tremble with joy. "The great tree! The great tree! I can see it from here!" she called out.

"B-b-but . . . but what's that?" Cuffyn asked, gesturing to dozens and dozens of owls flying toward them.

"Strix Struma Strikers!" Bell gasped, then blinked. "And the Flame Squadron, the Bonk Brigade with Bubo in the lead — and there's Doc Finebeak!"

Doc Finebeak split off from the tracking unit he was commanding. "Take over, Sylvana." He swiveled his head. "I'll catch up."

"It's little Bell!" A cheer from the Guardians roared up into the night.

"What's happening?" Cuffyn asked.

"It's war . . ." Doc Finebeak replied. "In the sixth kingdom." Then he seemed to notice the blue owl. "You're from there, aren't you?" The blue owl staggered in his flight.

"Yes," he said softly, and turned to Bell. "I lied, letting you think I was from the Northern Kingdoms. I didn't mean to."

"More important, you helped to save this little owl," Doc said. "Her mother was gizzard-broken."

Something swelled within the blue owl. "I can help you. I will get you to what you call the sixth kingdom. I know the way of the Zong Phong and how to fly through the hole in the wind."

"We were to seek someone called Bess, in the Shadow Forest," Doc Finebeak replied. "She was to tell us where this place is."

"No. I'll save you time. I will lead you there. I know the moonfaced owl has gone there. She is terrible."

"You needn't tell us!" Doc Finebeak said, then turned to Cuffyn. "Can you get this little one the rest of the way home?"

"Certainly."

"You're going, Striga?" Bell said, turning to the blue owl.

"I'll be back. I promise."

"How can I thank you?"

"You don't need to. I should thank you." *Yes*, thought this owl, once called Orlando and now called Striga. *I might have found the shortcut to the completion of my phonqua. It really does seem possible — at last.*

"But I want to do something for you," Bell protested.

The blue owl hovered and peered deeply into Bell's dark eyes. The pale yellow light seem to flood through Bell's hollow bones. "Just live purely and simply from the innermost part of your gizzard — the 'ryth,' as we owls of the Middle Kingdom, the kingdom of Jouzho, call it."

"You mean, no red berry decorations?"

The blue owl churred. "That's a start . . . that's a start," he said, and then began a steep banking turn to join the Guardian fighting units of the tree.

He was intoxicated with this new feeling that flowed through him and powered his flight. He felt a new alertness in his gizzard. It felt trim — trim and ready for the completion, the moment when the cycle was at last broken and his life would be a real life, not a travesty. A zeal burned through him. Now the lessons of the Danyar would be his. It was all about control, self-control, and through that, one could indeed become the master of one's fate.

CHAPTER TWENTY
Lessons of the Owlery

It is all in the breath, Twilight. You must first master the zong qui," the danyk said. She spoke decent Hoolian, but with a slight Krakish burr. This danyk was one of the five senior teachers of the Danyar — all of them female owls. "No move can be accomplished until you master the zong qui."

Twilight sighed. "This is the hardest battle trick I have ever tried. It's harder than working with those frinking ice splinters of the Frost Beaks."

"It is not a trick!" the danyk screeched. "That is what is wrong with you." She flew up and gave him a cuff that sent him flying across the hollow. "Why do you think we call this the Hollow of Extreme Concentration? We are not practitioners of cheap tricks. We fight bare-taloned with our minds and our gizzards. Why is the hollow of Danyar shaped like a gizzard? Now, before you can erect a zi field for combat, you must learn to breathe properly."

A small blue object whizzed by Twilight like the tail of a minuscule comet and slammed a much larger owl off its perch. It was a Pygmy Owl. Despite being blue, these owls did seem to be of a familiar species. The owl he had just knocked down seemed to be a Great Gray like Twilight — except he was blue. Twilight blinked. "What was that?" he asked.

"That was Pinyon," the danyk said, "executing a perfect third-degree Zi Kyan Mu."

Twilight had done this move before but wondered about the meaning of the words "third degree." "Third degree?" he asked.

"It simply means that he performed it with his talons turned in, so as not to kill."

"Oh." Twilight blinked. It was hard to imagine a Pygmy killing a Great Gray with nothing but his talons.

"Now back to the zong qui," the danyk ordered.

At first, Twilight had been surprised that the five senior danyks and many of the other teachers were female owls, but he was beginning to understand. In most owl species, females were larger than males. This would give the females an expanded lung capacity and since this breath was crucial to all the Danyar moves, it made sense that so many of the teachers were female. Very few other things, however, were making sense to Twilight.

Not the least confusing was why they refused to call this fighting, but "the way of noble gentleness." The art of Danyar was every bit as lethal as any battle claws or firebrands he had ever fought with. *Who're they trying to kid?* he thought. He was then knocked flat on his butt feathers. "You're not concentrating!" the danyk screeched. "Look at Ruby! She is concentrating. Beautiful focus." Ruby had just knocked an owl twice her size temporarily senseless.

Meanwhile, in another part of the owlery in the Hollow of Mental Cultivation, Otulissa, Digger, Soren, Gylfie, and Coryn sat with Mrs. Plithiver, huddled with the H'ryth, an owl who, with his featherless legs, most closely resembled a Burrowing Owl. He scratched his ya ni ni, which was the single blue feather that stuck up from the crown of his otherwise featherless head. It seemed to help him think. It was said that the ya ni ni was the point from which the zi emanated and created that incredible field of concentration and energy not just for action but for perception of other birds' zi fields. Every creature had such a field. A zi field, it was explained to the owls, radiates out from every animal. Some are good, some bad, some treacherous, but the pikyus of the owlery are trained to learn how to use their own and perceive others. The H'ryth was most impressed with Mrs. Plithiver's zi field. He said he had never seen anything comparable in a creature who was not a schooled pikyu of the owlery. He now gave his ya ni ni a bit of a jiggle.

"I have tried for so long to decipher the words of the eighth astrologer," the H'ryth said. "The papers that he wrote are so valuable, yet very obscure in their meaning."

"Can you explain," Otulissa asked, "why that astrologer left the Dragon Court?"

"Again, such things are difficult to explain. Our notions and ways are so strange to you. It was during the time of the eighth court that the first H'ryth, Theo — or Theosang, as he became known — came to this kingdom. He was alarmed by the devastation and the futility of war, but he found the Dragon Court an utterly foolish and useless place as well. But, and this is the genius of our first H'ryth, he found a purpose for this very useless court. The Dragon Court, with all its ridiculous extravagance and luxury, offered its owls a semblance of power. It could distract those who might seek power for the wrong reasons. Don't kill them with battle claws, kill them with luxury and splendor. It became a kind of prison, but one that was never called that by name. Theosang made it even more luxurious. He discouraged hunting by telling these owls that they were too fine for such lowly pursuits. Other owls would hunt for them. He provided servants to cater to their every whim. It was an incredibly clever way of distracting them and quelling the most dangerous elements that had begun to find their way into the Middle Kingdom after Theo had crossed the Sea of Vastness. The ancient evil ones, those who lusted for power — these were the ones Theosang committed to the Panqua Palace."

The ancient evil ones, Digger thought. *Hagsfiends?*

The H'ryth continued, "When the court changed with the arrival of Theosang, the last astrologer, the eighth one and the best, was only too happy to leave the palace and go to serve in the owlery, where Theosang was becoming a profoundly respected leader. This astrologer was gifted beyond belief. And during the time of Theosang he made many predictions. However, those predictions are most difficult to interpret."

Otulissa was at that very moment hunched and squinting over one of these documents. Occasionally, she would jot down a note on a piece of parchment.

Never had she concentrated so hard. In the sputtering light of the yak-butter lamp, she squinted at the letters. She could make out a few words. But they were like fragments of puzzles, and nothing seemed to fit. She raked through her memory for any old Krakish words that might relate. Otulissa prided herself on her skills of interpretation and logic, her great linguistical insights.

But she felt as if she was up against a wall here, an impenetrable wall. Reading the Theo Papers had been easy next to this. But the H'ryth felt it was a matter of some urgency that these writings of the eighth astrologer be understood. He perceived a threat, a danger that was imminent.

Otulissa bent closer to the paper. "And they will —" Her gizzard gave a twitch. At just that moment, Mrs. Plithiver coiled up and hissed. It was the nest-maid hiss of alarm. Two pikyus swooped into the Hollow of Mental Cultivation and announced something in rapid Jouzhen. The H'ryth turned to Coryn.

"Two owls from the west, a Barn Owl and a Pygmy, are flying this way with the red banner."

"The red banner?"

"The red banner from qui dong Tengshu. It can mean only one thing: We are about to be attacked!"

CHAPTER TWENTY-ONE

Zong Quí

Eglantine! Primrose!" Soren gasped as his sister swept down through the sky port into the library, the red streamer unfurled behind her. Primrose alighted near the parchment that Otulissa was attempting to decipher. They were both breathing heavily. Gasping and coughing, they gulped for air and tried to speak.

"Slink melf . . . Nyra . . ." Eglantine choked out.

Then Primrose took over. "They're on their way. They got to the River of Wind somehow . . . not from Bess . . ."

"Battle stations!" a pikyu commanded, and then the entire Mountain of Time reverberated with the sound of an immense gong.

"This way," the H'ryth shouted, and flew straight up to the port through which Eglantine and Primrose had just entered. The Chaw of Chaws was right behind him, and as they flew into the gusting winds they spied, surging over the last ranks of jagged peaks, twelve, perhaps fifteen owls, their battle claws glistening in the light of an almost full-shine moon.

Coryn's gizzard stilled. *It can't be. It can't be!* he thought. But it was. His mother, Nyra, her scarred moon face illuminated by the glare of the stars, flew through the slashing winds, her battle claws extended.

Soren blinked and drew in his breath sharply. He saw the glaring face as well. But there was something different yet eerily familiar about her face. One side of it shone with a truly blinding brilliance.

"It's the mask of Kludd!" Gylfie said, her voice cold with shock. "She is wearing the mask of Kludd!" Kludd, Nyra's mate and Coryn's father, had worn this metal mask to cover his battle-mutilated face. Why would she wear it? Had she been terribly injured? Coryn's memory reeled back in time to when he was a young owlet being raised by his widowed mother in the canyonlands. To a time when he was so young he did not know her evilness, to a time when he had believed that his uncle Soren had murdered his father. Coryn had attended the Final ceremonies in the cave where Kludd had been killed. He remembered it vividly. It was in the cave where they had burned his father's bones that he had discovered his ability to read fire and experienced his first insight of the flames that began to reveal the lies — all the lies that he had been told.

"It's a slink melf," Eglantine screed as she landed on a parapet of the owlery. "But we sent word to the great tree."

In the background, Coryn heard the almost tranquil voice of the H'ryth giving commands to his pikyus. Next to him, a member of the circle of the acolytes perched. These acolytes were the H'ryth's closest advisors. This one, a Spotted Owl, turquoise with deep midnight blue spots, translated. "The H'ryth will give the signal for zong qui and then the first of our Danyks will advance."

"We have no battle claws," Soren whispered.

"Yak butter!" Otulissa said, and swooped down to pluck one of the flaming brush torches.

"We use what we have," the H'ryth said. "The breath of qui, the butter of yak, and our fields of zi will converge."

There was a sudden gusting sound that was not dissimilar from the wind bong they had experienced on their way to the owlery when the winds had exploded through the notch in the mountains.

The senior danyk from the Danyar caught a glimpse of her stubborn pupil. *He's doing it,* she thought. *He's actually doing it!* Twilight had swelled to three times his size with the deep intake of one breath. He felt the zong qui flow through him. His gizzard seemed twice its normal size. He sensed a field of energy surrounding him. And did he feel a buzz or humming?

"Extend coal claws," Nyra screed.

How have they gotten coal claws? Soren wondered. Coal claws were the most dangerous of all battle claws. In each tip, a bonk coal burned. The Pure Ones advanced upon them now, the claws glowing red with a tinge of blue — hot fangs in the night.

Fight fire with fire, Soren thought, and inhaled deeply. He was no master of the zong qui but he did feel himself fly very fast. "Grip, split, and roll," he shouted. It was a strategic maneuver to divide an attacking unit, particularly useful when that unit had superior weapons. The butter torches seemed made for this job.

"Eeeyawk," Twilight cried as he saw Nyra spin out. "I'm going to put that mask where it belongs!" he shrieked.

"Do not waste breath of zong qui, young one," said the danyk who, with a tail move, had severed a Pure One's wing. A quick death. The glowing talon trailed a wake of sparks as the owl plummeted down into the icy gorge. Twilight, inspired, curled his own talon into the shape known as the deadly blossom. He was on the tail of a Grass Owl who was flying very fast. *Concentrate,* Twilight told himself. *Concentrate!* The Grass Owl suddenly wheeled about in midair. The glowing claws were coming straight toward him. Twilight dodged and heard a crash behind him. It was the danyk. The Grass Owl plunged toward the ground. "I could have gotten him! I could have!" Twilight shouted.

"Save breath, stupid one!" the danyk barked, and flew off.

From a spire high on the owlery, Mrs. Plithiver perceived the battle. She did not need to see to know what was transpiring. Every sensory fiber in her body was grasping the most minute details. Feathers flew through the air along with detached fire claws. It seemed as if the Pure Ones were losing their edge in this battle despite their numbers. She began calling out commands to the Hoolian owls. She did not know the ways of the Danyar but she knew her owls, the ones of the great tree. She knew their skills and how they fought. "A flying wedge, keep torches down, now loft and hurl." The commands she had just shouted out were for a classic rocket maneuver that the Bonk Brigade often used. The owls worked in teams of two. One owl launched the flaming missile, in this case torches. The second owl retrieved it after the target had been hit. It took incredible skill and cooperation. Soren had invented it.

The Chaw of Chaws was being very effective right now, but then Mrs. P. began to perceive something profoundly disturbing. Were they about to lose that edge?

"Oh, Great Glaux." The rocket maneuver was backfiring. Nyra had lured the two-owl team of Soren and Coryn, uncle and nephew, into an indefensible situation. Mrs. P. couldn't see it, but she knew it. She felt a great stirring in the air. *More Guardians*, she thought. They would now outnumber the Pure Ones. Nyra's own losses were mounting. But did it matter? The slink melf was with her. The whole purpose of this battle, Mrs. P. suddenly realized, was not to destroy all the Guardians but to assassinate just two.

"It's the Frost Beaks, the Flame Squadron! They're coming!" Ruby cried out. *It doesn't matter*, thought Mrs. Plithiver. *Not if they only want Soren and Coryn.* She knew in the spiraling bones of her spine that Nyra did not care about the lives of her followers but only sought the death of her own son and his uncle, the brother of her mate, Kludd, whose mask she now wore.

Soren swerved in his pursuit of Nyra. He kept the torch low. Coryn flanked his starboard wing, ready to dive at the moment of launch. Nyra was heading toward a break in a cliff. They were closing the gap. Just before the notch, she ducked down, reversing her direction. But the king and his uncle worked smoothly together. No words were exchanged. They knew instinctively how to maneuver. They pivoted, hovered, and dove. The torch whistled out. But then something flew from the notch, pressing them back against the ice face. It was a Pure Ones' captain. He caught the torch on the fly. Four Pure Ones now advanced on them. *How did we get outmaneuvered? I should have known!* Coryn thought, and made a wild dive. But the slink melf was on him. Nyra was howling and called him by his hatchling name. "You had your chance, Nyroc! You had it. Now, what'll it be? The ember or your life?"

Soren now had nothing — no torch, no battle claws, nothing. He saw a reddish streak. *Ruby? Ruby and Twilight?*

Save your breath, Twilight, save your breath, the Great Gray cautioned himself, but in his head a chant began. *Tore your face once, tore it twice, going to smash you up with that ice . . .* The chant dwindled. He could not even think it. He had to concentrate . . . *concentrate.* Ruby had the torch. He would try the Zi Phan, the talon like the spiked flower. He spread the four talons of each foot as far as he could. He knew the power came from the downstroke. He felt his zi begin to tingle and was about to strike.

He would get her — get Nyra once and for all. He opened his beak. "Eeeyrrrrk!" The terrible sound tore the clouds from the sky, shattered the light of the moon, peeled the ice from a cliff. There was another blur of blue! A blue owl Twilight had never seen before. Had that terrible sound come from this owl's throat or his own?

Twilight was confused. Then he saw Nyra lurch in flight. The blue owl hurled himself toward the slink melf. Feathers spun through the air. Blood — so much blood! The ice cliff was streaked with blood. Something bright and shining went flying through the air and there was a metallic clank below. Then silence, a profound silence. Even the wind seemed to have stopped. Soren, Twilight, Ruby, and Coryn alighted on a bloody shelf.

"They're gone, I think," Ruby said.

"Look down. There are bodies," Soren said, breathing heavily. Blood spread in the snow, and in the midst of the red glared a bright metal mask.

"Great Glaux, it's her!" Soren exclaimed. The four owls lifted into flight and began to hover in descending circles over the carnage. A few seconds later, they landed.

"So much blood," Twilight said. "I thought these fellows were not about blood. The danyk said that to tear with talons was considered an ignoble way to win at combat."

They looked at one another, perplexed. "Who did this?" Coryn asked.

"Oh, no." Soren was slowly walking around the slaughtered owls. Gingerly, he put out his talons and turned the blood-streaked mask over. There was no face beneath it. "There are only three bodies."

"She got away?" Twilight said.

"I tried," a voice spoke quietly. It was the blue owl, the one who had so suddenly appeared.

"You tried," the danyk swooped down. "You call this trying? This is an affront to the entire meaning of Danyar, the way of noble gentleness. This is ignoble."

The blue owl wilfed. "I am not ignoble. I am not!" He wept. Other owls were gathering. The pikyus gasped in shock at the blood, the torn wings. "It's death, isn't it?" the blue owl asked in a trembling voice tinged with desperation.

The H'ryth alighted. "It is death unclean, death with greatest pain. You acted selfishly. You did not kill but murdered. You struck those fatal bloody blows not from the innermost part of your gizzard but from your pride and your anger."

"But Holy One," the blue owl now collapsed before the H'ryth, "I have done honorable things."

"He has," Doc Finebeak said. "He rescued Bell."

"Bell?" Soren said. "Bell — what happened to Bell?" Then it came back to him. The terrible dream he had had at the Panqua Palace. That urgency that had coursed through him in his sleep, the feeling that he had to return immediately, that someone very dear to him was in danger.

He blinked at the owl and remembered the blue feather that had in his dream floated near the desert floor.

"She is fine now. She is safe, thanks to this blue owl," Doc Finebeak said. "And not only that, he guided us here."

The H'ryth winced at the word "guided." "He is no pikyu!" the H'ryth spoke harshly. "He is an escaped dragon owl."

"What?" The Guardians looked nervously at one another and began to mumble among themselves.

"But he saved an owlet," Soren said passionately. "He saved my daughter."

"Phonqua byrmong ping tsay phrak." Slowly, as the H'ryth spoke, the words formed meaning in Otulissa's mind.

"He says this owl believes he has broken the wheel of life, has made a shortcut to change his fate," she translated the speech softly to the others.

"I have . . . I have . . ." the blue owl said in a shrill voice.

"You are still Orlando," the H'ryth spoke now in Hoolian.

"Call him what you will, but he is a good and decent owl," Soren continued to protest. Orlando seemed to swell a bit from his wilfed state.

"I thought his name was Striga," Doc Finebeak said.

A new light burned in the blue owl's eyes. "The Striga," he said softly.

The H'ryth felt a deep agonizing twinge in his gizzard. He turned his gaze on the dragon owl. "You are still a dragon owl. Time will tell if you have satisfied your fate, your phonqua."

"May he come with us?" Coryn asked.

The H'ryth turned to address them. "You are all noble owls. We have expected you for hundreds of years. And we have the deepest respect for you. We see in you many of the traits of our beloved Theo, our first H'ryth. We have all tried to live up to the values that the first H'yrth, Theosang, taught and practiced. We know you do not understand phonqua, but we do understand that Orlando has proven valuable to you. He is not a noble owl. Nor is he in this phase of phonqua an evil one. It is your decision if he is to go with you to the great tree. But know this: His phonqua has not been satisfied, has not come full circle." With that, the H'ryth spread his wings. Slowly, majestically, he rose in the air and soared above the icy peaks, spiraling higher and higher until he reached the highest hollow of the Mountain of Time.

CHAPTER TWENTY-TWO

Home

The Aurora Glaucora was playing across the sky as the returning owls flew across the Sea of Hoolemere. All the owls of the tree would be out frolicking in the colors that washed the night.

"Like banners! Like the tails of the qui," Ruby said as she caught sight of the undulating waves' light.

"More beautiful, I am sure," Mrs. Plithiver spoke, and tilted her head toward the shimmering, shifting lights of the night sky. It was as if she could sense every drop of color.

"Pelli!" Soren cried out as he spotted his beloved mate, and behind her in the folds of color that swayed in the sky, three young owlets flew. "Da! Da!" It was Bell, who rushed ahead of her two sisters.

"Da!" she shreed, then turned to the blue owl. "Striga, you came back. You came back."

"Of course I did, little Bell."

Although tired, the returning owls joined the others

and wove themselves through the pulsating banners of color for the rest of the night until the dawn crept over the horizon.

"Death of night," Soren said to himself.

"What's that, dear?" Pelli asked as they headed back to their hollow.

"Oh, it's just an expression of the sixth kingdom. They don't call it twixt time and tweener or First Black, but death of day for night and death of night for day, or sometimes the hatch of night. I like that."

"Oh, yes," Pelli replied thoughtfully. "They see it as a kind of cycle that goes in a circle."

"Yes, they speak that way. The wheel of life is another expression."

"Wheel . . . I saw a wheel once, or part of one, I think. Trader Mags brought it shortly after I first came here. They say it just goes around and around in endless circles. Seems rather pointless, doesn't it? Wheel of life. I can't imagine."

Soren shook his head. No, she could never imagine. In his gizzard, he felt the dimmest tremor as he thought of phonqua and the blue owl who had saved his dear little Bell. The three B's were already sound asleep. He peered out the port of their hollow. Pink-and-orange light streaked the morning and the Sea of Hoolemere glittered fiercely. *It all seems rather . . . rather . . .* Pelli was looking at him. She sensed what he was thinking.

"Rather tawdry and cheap, isn't it, after the delicate colors of the Aurora Glaucora?" she said.

"My thoughts exactly," Soren churred. "It truly is the death of night, isn't it?"

"But night will return — just like the wheel of life," Pelli said.

"Yes, like the wheel of life."

"Mum," a small voice called. "Can I have a drink of water?" It was Blythe.

"Me, too," said Bash. "I want one, too."

But Bell slept on peacefully, dreamless and simply content, safely tucked into the soft nest made from Mum's and Da's downiest feathers.

OWLS
and others
from the

GUARDIANS OF GA'HOOLE SERIES

The Band

SOREN: Barn Owl, *Tyto alba*, from the Forest Kingdom of Tyto; escaped from St. Aegolius Academy for Orphaned Owls; a Guardian at the Great Ga'Hoole Tree and close advisor to the king

GYLFIE: Elf Owl, *Micranthene whitneyi*, from the desert kingdom of Kuneer; escaped from St. Aegolius Academy for Orphaned Owls; Soren's best friend; a Guardian at the Great Ga'Hoole Tree and ryb of navigation chaw

TWILIGHT: Great Gray Owl, *Strix nebulosa*, free flier; orphaned within hours of hatching; Guardian at the Great Ga'Hoole Tree

DIGGER: Burrowing Owl, *Athene cunicularia*, from the desert kingdom of Kuneer; lost in desert after attack in which his brother was killed by owls from St. Aegolius; a Guardian at the Great Ga'Hoole Tree

The Leaders of the Great Ga'Hoole Tree

CORYN: Barn Owl, *Tyto alba*, the new young king of the great tree; son of Nyra, leader of the Pure Ones

EZYLRYB: Whiskered Screech Owl, *Otus trichopsis*, Soren's former mentor; the wise, much-loved, departed ryb at the Great Ga'Hoole Tree

Others at the Great Ga'Hoole Tree

OTULISSA: Spotted Owl, *Strix occidentalis*, chief ryb and ryb of Ga'Hoology and weather chaws; an owl of great learning and prestigious lineage

MARTIN: Northern Saw-whet Owl, *Aegolius acadicus*, member of the Chaw of Chaws; a Guardian at the Great Ga'Hoole Tree

RUBY: Short-eared Owl, *Asio flammeus*, member of the Chaw of Chaws; a Guardian at the Great Ga'Hoole Tree

EGLANTINE: Barn Owl, *Tyto alba*, Soren's younger sister

MADAME PLONK: Snowy Owl, *Nyctea scandiaca*, the elegant singer of the Great Ga'Hoole Tree

MRS. PLITHIVER: blind snake, formerly the nest-maid for Soren's family; now a member of the harp guild at the Great Ga'Hoole Tree

PELLI: Barn Owl, *Tyto alba*, Soren's mate

PRIMROSE: Pygmy Owl, *Glaucidium californicum*, Eglantine's best friend

OCTAVIA: Kielian snake, nest-maid for many years for Madame Plonk and Ezylryb (also known as BRIGID)

DOC FINEBEAK: Snowy Owl, *Nyctea scandiaca*, famed free-lance tracker once in the employ of the Pure Ones, now at the great tree; Madame Plonk's companion

Characters from the Time of the Legends

GRANK: Spotted Owl, *Strix occidentalis*, the first collier; friend to young King H'rath and Queen Siv during their youth; first owl to find the ember

HOOLE: Spotted Owl, *Strix occidentalis*, son of H'rath; retriever of the ember of Hoole; founder and first king of the great tree

H'RATH: Spotted Owl, *Strix occidentalis*, king of the N'yrthghar, a frigid region known in later times as the Northern Kingdoms; father of Hoole

SIV: Spotted Owl, *Strix occidentalis*, mate of H'rath and Queen of the N'yrthghar, a frigid region known in later times as the Northern Kingdoms; mother of Hoole

KREETH: Female hagsfiend with strong powers of nacht-magen; friend of Ygryk; conjures Lutta into being

Other Characters

NYRA: Barn Owl, *Tyto alba*, leader of the Pure Ones; Coryn's mother

STRYKER: Barn Owl, *Tyto alba*, a commander of the Pure Ones under Nyra

GYLLBANE: courageous member of the MacHeath clan of dire wolves; her pup, Cody, was maimed by clan leader Dunleavy MacHeath

BESS: Boreal Owl, *Aegolius funerus*, daughter of Grimble, who was a guard at St. Aegolius Academy for Orphaned Owls; keeper of the Palace of Mists (also known as THE KNOWER)

Blue Owls

STRIGA: Blue Snowy Owl, *Nyctea scandiaca*, a former dragon owl from the Middle Kingdom seeking a more meaningful life (also known as ORLANDO)

TENGSHU: Blue Long-eared Owl, *Asio otis*, qui master and sage of the Middle Kingdom

Coming soon!

GUARDIANS OF GA'HOOLE

BOOK FOURTEEN

Exile

by Kathryn Lasky

The unthinkable has happened! The Band is banished from the Great Ga'Hoole Tree. Slowly, inexorably, the Striga, a mysterious blue owl from the Middle Kingdom, has gained control over young Coryn's mind and exiled his closest friends and advisors — Soren, Gylfie, Twilight, and Digger — from the tree. The Striga institutes a harsh new regime that will not stop until learning itself — the very foundation of the tree — becomes suspect and books are consigned to flame. Somehow the Band must open Coryn's eyes to the Striga's malign influence. But how? They are in exile!

About the Author

KATHRYN LASKY has had a long fascination with owls. Several years ago, she began doing extensive research about these birds and their behaviors — what they eat, how they fly, how they build or find their nests. She thought that she would someday write a nonfiction book about owls illustrated with photographs by her husband, Christopher Knight. She realized, though, that this would indeed be difficult since owls are nocturnal creatures, shy and hard to find. So she decided to write a fantasy about a world of owls. But even though it is an imaginary world in which owls can speak, think, and dream, she wanted to include as much of their natural history as she could.

Kathryn Lasky has written many books, both fiction and nonfiction, including *Sugaring Time*, for which she won a Newbery Honor. Among her fiction books are *The Night Journey*, a winner of the National Jewish Book Award; and *Beyond the Burning Time*, an ALA Best Book for Young Adults. She has also received The Boston Globe / Horn Book Award as well as The Washington Post Children's Book Guild Award for her contribution to nonfiction.

Lasky and her husband live in Cambridge, Massachusetts.